By Barry Unsworth

THE IDOL HUNTER

Barry Unsworth

SIMON AND SCHUSTER
NEW YORK

I should like to thank the Arts Council of Great Britain for their grant of a Creative Writing Fellowship for the year 1978–79, in the course of which a great part of this novel was written; and the Principal and staff of the Charlotte Mason College, Ambleside, Cumbria, where my Fellowship was held, for their kindness and support during my stay there.

LIBRARY OF CONGRESS CATALOGING IN PUBLICATION DATA
UNSWORTH, BARRY, DATE.
THE IDOL HUNTER.
PREVIOUS ED. PUBLISHED UNDER TITLE: PASCALI'S ISLAND.
I. TITLE.
PZ4.U59ID [PR6071.N8] 823'.914 80–14989
ISBN 0–671–25357–3

TO JACK AND SHEILA CARTER

Nothingness might save or destroy those who face it, but those who ignore it are condemned to unreality.

—*Demetrius Capetanakis*

Lord of the world. Shadow of God on earth. God bring you increase.

You do not know me, Excellency. I am your paid informer on this island. One of them at least, for there may be others. Forgive this temerity of your creature in addressing you. I am driven to it. I can no longer endure the neglect of your officials. In spite of repeated humble requests no word has come to me from the Ministry, no single word of acknowledgment. Never. Not from the beginning. Twenty years, Excellency. I sit here at my table, in the one room of my house above the shore, on this island, far from Constantinople and the centers of power. I have calculated that this is my two hundred and sixteenth report.

It promises to be my last. The Greeks know. I have suspected it for some time, there have been indications, but it was only this morning, not three hours ago, that I became convinced of it, at the quayside, just after the Englishman had disembarked.

They know. I saw it on the face of old Dranas this morning.

Everything the same: pain of neglect; sea and shore outside my window; benign sea light on the few words already written and the blank pages waiting, on my plump, short-fingered, inoffensive hands. Yet everything changed. It may take days or weeks but I am as good as dead. Undeservedly. No one has ever suffered as a result of my reports. Now I am in the open, soft-skinned, like the crucified man. (I saw a man who had been crucified, when I was a child, in Scutari.)

9

How can I bear to die without acknowledgments? My million words dropped one by one into silence. Why?

I ask the same questions. Is it that I am too verbose? My style, is it too complicated or obscure? I am aware that my reports have become more copious over the years, but there has been so much, so much to write about, Excellency. Everything, anything, may be important—may be vital. Inflections of a voice, gradations in the light, changes in the weather—where are we to draw the line?

This time, at least, I have something important to begin with. (Important to me, I mean, Excellency: my life and death are equally insignificant in your eyes. You view me as I view the small fly at present entangled in the hairs on the back of my left hand.) I mean the arrival of the Englishman. Important because he came *today;* because with his arrival came a glimpse of my death; because I felt then some linking of our destinies.

His name is A. Bowles. This was the name on his luggage, and the name under which he registered at the hotel. He arrived at midday, on the *Marmaris.* Coming from Smyrna, Excellency. He is staying at the Hotel Metropole on the *plateia.* All the foreigners stay there. It is the best hotel on the island. It is the only hotel on the island. According to Yannis, the porter there (a one-eyed man, very morose), he is staying for an indefinite period. The hotel is owned by an Armenian, named Mardosian, who has featured several times in my reports, because of his connections with certain disaffected elements in Salonika, that breeding ground of freemasons and revolutionaries. They think, the Armenians that is, and Mardosian among them, that their race would be more humanely treated by the Young Turks than by your Excellency's Kurdish irregulars. Quite possibly they are right.

I saw the Englishman disembark. I was there, on the quay, as I am every Wednesday at that time. I saw him standing on the deck. He was looking toward the land, toward us. A tall figure in fawn-colored suit and paler hat. Straight shoulders.

Again misgivings assail me. Are these things really important, details of dress and manner? I would like to tell you everything: the hue of seasons, stirrings of my heart and mind, the speech and behavior—treasonable or otherwise—of your subjects, whether Greek, Turk, Armenian or Jew, whether believer or *ghiaour*; and of the European residents, who are usually neither. Everything. Then I should be the ideal, the Platonic Form of an informer. But we are finite creatures, though boundless in ambition.

I pause to consider the predicament of the tiny, amber-colored fly entrapped in the fronds of my wrist hairs. At the base of the hairs, faint shine of moisture. The fly struggles and swoons in this swamp, amidst the miasmic exudations of my skin. (I use the present tense here, Excellency, for the sake of vividness, and because of the brief interval between observing and recording.) In fact there is no fly, no actual fly. The fly belongs to the realm of fancy. Useful, though: serving as an image of my insignificance in your eyes; symbolically entangled in my hairs, as I am entangled in language; and possessing essential truth—flies expire, as spies perspire, on this island as throughout your domains. You see what purposes are served by this fly, which does not exist?

You could not have known this, Excellency, if I had not chosen to tell you. You could not have known about the fly. I, your creature, imposed an idea on you. My only power. But perhaps you do know. Perhaps you know everything. What if, after all these years in which no acknowledgment came, years in which my sense of impunity gradually flowered into art, into control of illusion, making me see myself and the island and the people on it as things which in my reports I could *create*, what if all the time I was merely confirming what was already sensed, felt, known—my detection and death included?

No. I must for my sanity's sake assume there are things unknown to you. Like the precise aspect of the world outside my window, composed of sky and sea and shore. Let me describe it to you. At this time of afternoon, the shore is always deserted. No sound from the sea, no sound from the

11

town rising on its slopes behind me. (My house is down near the shore, Excellency, away from the main part of the town. One room inside and a square stone terrace with a trellised vine. I rent it from Christopheros the grocer.)

At present because of the slight haze or graining in the air, only the nearer islands are visible: Spargos with its almost symmetrical bulk, the long jagged line of Ramni. Below me I can follow the sweep of the bay as far as the headland, and see beyond to the pale heights of the mainland, across the straits. In this thickening of atmosphere, the sand and stones of the shore appear slightly smoky, as if enveloped thinly in their own breath. Beyond this the sea is opaline, gashed near the horizon by a long, gleaming line of light. The light fumes upward into the sky. The American's caïque will be somewhere out there, lying in that gash of light. (I referred briefly to this American at the end of my last report. He has been here ten days now, fishing for sponges. He has a crew of three: two divers—Italians—and another man, who does not often come ashore. They say he is a Pole or a Russian.)

I must return to Mister Bowles. I ought to have returned to him earlier, but felt reluctant—perhaps because I am afraid of failing with him: he is vital to the success of this report. How can I make sure you have a true picture of his arrival? You will know these island harbors. This day no different from others. The boat at first no more than a slightly darker speck, a small imperfection, in the glimmering line of the horizon, assuming shape from minute to minute; finally unmistakably what we were gathered there for: the little packet steamer, blistered white and blue, two strings of bunting across the upper deck, S.S. *Marmaris*, Gavros et Fils, Smyrna.

Mister Bowles assumed definition along with the boat. Distinguishable while yet a good way off by his tallness, and the light clothes. I watched him, the boat meanwhile nosing into harbor and the water slapping, vegetable matter eddying between hulk and moorings.

He remained standing at the rail, looking at the town rising before him on its terraced slopes. The hat shadowed his face. And now something very strange, Excellency: I began to see the town through the eyes of this newcomer; somehow he imposed his view on me—even before we met. Some unshakable confidence he managed to convey, or perhaps simply indifference to the assessments of others. Whatever the reason, I was constrained to look up as if for the first time, to note the white houses with their shallow roofs and ramshackle storks' nests, the whole town enmeshed in the green of its terraces, the minarets of mosques and the broken towers of the Frankish castle sticking up through the net, brown falcons loitering in the sky above.

He came down the gangway. A sailor carried his two brown leather bags. He carried a smaller bag himself. He has a fair moustache, not drooping—ending at the corners of his mouth. His face is sunburned. A longish, rather thin face, pale narrow eyes—the eyes seem paler because of his tan. He paused on the quay, amid a little group of people competing for his attention—*fiacre*-drivers, children clamoring for *kurus*, *hammals* eager to carry his luggage on their backs. He took off his hat, for some reason, quite unhurriedly. His hair is brown, darker than the moustache, and smooth, parted down the middle. He holds himself stiffly, but there is something less than assured in his movements, a quality of diffidence or slight uncertainty, rather graceful in its effect. At that moment, as he stood there alone and bareheaded, at that moment, I felt the importance of his arrival for me. (Even before old Dranas set the seal on it.) And again he imposed his experience on me—the voices of those around him, the reek of the *fiacre* horses, the squabbling drivers in their black skullcaps and dirty calico. (The drivers are all Greeks, Excellency, noted for their powers of invective.)

I was moving forward, with the intention of offering help, when he looked toward me and our eyes met for a brief moment. Then he looked away, made his own compact with one of those besieging him—Dranas, it was—and they moved off together to where his cab was waiting, under the eucalyptus adjoining the quay.

I followed them into the town. On foot, of course—my pay does not permit much indulgence in *fiacres*. On the outskirts of town flocks of penned sheep, marked with red, reminded me again that this is the twelfth month of the Moslem year, and Sacrifice *Bayram* falls next week. The hillsides near the town are loud with the cries of these sheep. I could still faintly hear them as I approached the main *plateia*.

Dranas was still there, sitting up on his cab, on the corner near the Metropole. He looked down at me without expression.

I need not have spoken to him at all, Excellency. I was sure in any case that the Englishman had been taken to the Metropole. Perhaps it was the blankness of his face that made me speak. I asked after his health and that of his family—he has two grandchildren now, both boys. To these inquiries he replied curtly, scratching his gray stubble, watching my face without a smile. And this in itself was strange. I am a well-known figure on the island; children call out after me; everyone has a word and a smile for me. They know me, Excellency: Basil Pascali, plump and good-humored; shabby, but with a certain dash—the ruby ring my stepfather gave me, my monogrammed handkerchiefs. I am derided, but not disliked. Or so I thought, until today.

Jokingly I said, "I hope you did not overcharge the Englishman?"

Such a remark would normally have been greeted with some play-acting, slyly exaggerated assertions of honesty. But Dranas did not even smile. "From the harbor to the *plateia* it is twenty-five *kurus*," he said. "Everyone knows that."

"I know it," I said, in the same manner as before. "And you know it. But does he?"

For only answer the old ruffian leaned forward and spat sideways. The spittle landed quite near my left shoe. This is a sign of hostility and contempt among uneducated Greeks, Excellency, and although still puzzled I decided to move away. I knew now that the Englishman was staying at the Metropole. I was turning away when Dranas spoke again. "If there are complaints," he said, "I will know who to thank."

"Complaints?" I said. "I make no complaints. It is none of my business. Why are you speaking to me in this way?"

Dranas looked at me and moved his head up and down slightly, several times. "*Xerome ti isse*" he said. "We know."

I was frightened by his face. It was so vindictive and so *certain*. No matter if in his ignorance he reduces my role to his own scale, to questions of cab-fares, a few *kurus* more or less. He knows what I am. And if he, others—whose scale will be different.

We exchanged a long glance. For that shocked moment, as I looked into the old man's face, everything hushed, stopped. Then suddenly, without cover and soft-skinned as I was, exhilaration swept through me, the sense of a desired ending, and I smiled full at old Dranas. I smiled broadly, saying nothing, and I saw his face change. Then I turned and walked away.

Now, however, back in my room, fear returns. Fear of the void to which I am moving. My words, the motion of my hand as it writes, alike proceeding to the void. Parmenides knew this, spent his life denying it, constructed a system of philosophy, founded a school, attempting to deny void and motion alike as illusory. The universe perpetually brim-full. Is not your Excellency's foreign policy, holding together a crumbling Empire, based on fear of the void? For twenty years I have poured language in, trying to achieve a depth which would enable me to drown. . . .

The sea is blank. Without mark or indentation anywhere. A fitting image for the void. Intractable matter, indifferent to suffering and aspiration. At least in these pages of mine there is possibility of spirit and form. This July weather is hot. The insides of my thighs prickle along the line of their junction. My hookah and cushion in the corner. Or perhaps sleep for a little, not too long, then resume later. My eyes give me trouble these days.

If only I could come in person to Stamboul, I would sit day and night in the anterooms of the Ministry until I obtained audience with Mehmet Bey. He it was who directed me to this island, twenty years ago. Twenty years, Excellency! He would be able to explain things to me. For all I know, my reports, though never acknowledged, are being used elsewhere in your vast dominions. But for every step in those corridors *bakhshish* would be needed. Perhaps your Excellency is not aware to what extent the wheels of your administration are lubricated by bribes? And I am poor. I can barely live on my pay. It comes regularly, I do not complain about that, but it has not increased in all the years I have been here, despite rising prices. There are days when I cannot afford coffee or tobacco. There are days when I do not eat. Besides, my will has been sapped. I do not believe that either fear or ambition will get me off this island now. There is only my room, the words on the page. I will sit here while they talk themselves into murdering me. Perhaps I can hold off fear of death and dissolution by making my existence real to you, re-creating my substance, as it were. I will withhold nothing, Excellency. I will give my whole time to this report—I have nothing else to do. . . .

I must not change the Englishman into a *character*, as I have done so often with others. I must in what I write of him keep to observed truth—aided of course by reasonable inference and imaginative insight. (We are nowhere without this latter.)

He looked at me briefly, our eyes met. His eyes look as if they ought to recognize you, but don't, and are angry, or perhaps merely puzzled, at this failure of recognition.

I slept, Excellency. Late in the afternoon now, judging by the sun. I no longer possess a watch, having been obliged by my necessities to sell it to Eskenazi three months ago. He gave me a quarter of its value. If this goes on I shall have to sell my telescope—which an Italian gentleman left behind.

Actually, I stole it from him. I will not sell my ring or my hookah or my books.

The sea has changed, taken on a new aspect with the shift of the sun. The blue is deeper, harder. Little trace now of that earlier haze. As if those opalescent particles had sunk below the surface, thickening the water. Sea and sky mingle no longer, ruled apart on the horizon. Later again this line will dissolve. I know every mood, every aspect of the sea. After all, I have been recording these details for twenty years. No, it is not so long. In my earlier years I did not concern myself with such matters, but concentrated strictly on the doings of the inhabitants: arrivals and departures, conversations, the activities of the Literary Society. They were meager and brief, those first reports. It was only gradually that I discovered my gift, realized that I had stumbled on my true métier. Then I began to see the island in its entirety as my subject. It is that which has kept me here, Excellency, in this one room, eking out a bare existence, deprived of all that makes life worth living for the many. The only concession to flesh my long-sustained fantasies about Lydia Neuman, an artist living here. That and my fortnightly visits to Ali, the mulatto boy at the baths. For the rest, observing, listening, writing. Writing. I have written my life away here.

No, the sea is not a proper image for the void. The sea is sufficiently inhabited with bodies both native and foreign—it doesn't matter which, as the sea makes everything its own, modifies everything in the interests of unity. This is exactly what the informer does, Excellency, with the elements he takes from life. Bleach, bloat, shimmer or rot—depending on the original substance. The sea is more strictly comparable to my finished report—multiplicity of effect within a single organic whole. . . .

While I am thus eagerly dreaming of my finished report, Hassan, the shore fisherman, emerges from the shadow of the café verandah farther along the shore toward the town. In the distance I see him stepping on legs thin as stilts down toward the sea. He holds his net like a gathered skirt. Stippled briefly by the bars of shadow cast by the verandah railing, he walks slowly toward me, out onto the vacant expanse of shore, keeping close to the sea. He is as I see him every day: beak of a nose turned steadily seaward, faded headcloth and ragged shirt, black *shalvar* tucked up above his crane's thighs. The same. Yet today, in this my last report, he seems like some special emissary or messenger. The universe is crammed with symbols and portents, for those who have eyes.

How did they find out about me? No one has been here in my absence, my papers have not been disturbed. Perhaps some casual indiscretion in Constantinople, reaching the wrong ears. Or the agent for the Banque Ottomane, where I go every month for my stipend, Mister Pariente . . . But he knows nothing of the source of the money. In any case, why now, after twenty years?

Nevertheless, some connection must have been made. There is a good deal of tension now on the island, with the rebels in the mountains stepping up activities. Separatist movements are everywhere gaining strength. I am not pure Greek, of course, they know that. I spend a lot of time with foreigners. All this might be regarded as suspicious. And then, two years ago, I ceased through boredom and laziness to attend the meetings of the Literary Society, where local patriots devote themselves to keeping Greek culture alive, quote Palamas and Pericles, express treasonable sentiments under the tutelage of the *pappas*. Harmless for the most part, but they have connections, Excellency; these thin threads of sentiment and subversion extend to the furthest corners of your possessions, and at points within this complex web are men with guns and money and friends abroad. My failure to attend may have gone against me.

I have continued to send details of these meetings, of course, even though not actually present at them. Why should it matter, when both fact and invention are received in silence? In solitude such as mine these distinctions blur. Even before I left the Society, many of those attending had become in my reports partially fictitious, or they were people culled from other times and other places, put in for the sake of color and variety.

Hassan is wading circumspectly into the pale water, holding the net stealthily above the surface. The water is so clear that I can see the glimmer of his legs below the surface. He stops, turns away sharply as if piqued with the sea, then at once makes his cast, swinging round again, ending with arms outstretched like a suppliant. The net sails out, bunched at first, catching sun in its strands and weights. It opens, glinting, resembling for this brief time a sudden gauzy swarm of insects over the sea. It drops, dipping its mesh into the water with the briefest glitter of disturbance.

Because the times I shall watch Hassan are numbered now, his actions take on ritual significance for me, a kind of lustral character. As do those of the group of women now sitting against the low wall at the top of the beach between here and the café. Dressed in black for bereavement and gossip. I can hear the plaintive, plangent notes of their voices. Movements, voices—timeless, immemorial. The island does not change. Mister Bowles saw it as the first colonizers must have seen it.

Why has he come, why is he here? An indefinite stay—that, in itself, is suspicious. If it were simply to see the castle built by the Crusaders, the Roman harbor installations, the Seljuk mosque, the classical remains along the coast, then two days and a guide would be sufficient. No, he has some other purpose in mind. "I hope you gave him a good room," I said to Yannis, who is bad-tempered, but a simple man. "Of course," he said, "Room 16, the big one, with a view of the sea." So I know where he is. Yannis did not seem more unfriendly than usual. Strange.

Hassan is a good way off along the shore. I see him again involved in that controlled violence of movement. The net invisible now, but the gesture unvarying, that final stillness of the outstretched arms. Beyond him the sea is wrinkled like the back of a hand. A thin moon above it. The fishing boats stand out in the bay, waiting for darkness. Further out I see the pale lights of the American's caïque, though not the shape of the boat itself.

Mister Bowles will be there now, in his room. Sitting at his window reviewing the events of the day, questioning himself, his motives. Or unpacking: perhaps a woman's photograph he always carries with him. No, he is writing in his journal—all English travelers have journals; it is an essential part of their equipment. He is making an entry in his journal before dinner. The English are very methodical and have a strong sense of duty, which they regard as sufficient morality. Wrongly.

Darkness is falling as he finishes his entry. He stands at the window of his room looking out. He hears, as I am hearing now, the wail of the muezzin calling on us to pray. Behind him faint crepitations. At once, with his strongly developed sense of hygiene, he suspects filthy cockroaches. From the *lokanta* across the square the sound of a zither. Someone singing a few words. Cooking smells. In a few moments he will go down to the dining room: plum-colored carpeting, oval tables, gilt chairs. Soft flares of the gas lamps along the walls. Biron, the waiter, slim and assiduous. Would monsieur like an apéritif? One of the tables on the terrace, perhaps? From here you can see the lights of the harbor.

I too must leave soon, if I am to get there before dinner. I intend to introduce myself to Mister Bowles, exert my charm, establish friendly relations.

Some domestic details now, Excellency, at the risk of being tedious. I want you to see me here in this room. I want you to see how your informers live. First a quick wash of hands and face, in cold water—my house, though convenient in many ways, being private and cheap, has certain disadvantages, among which is the absence of running water. I have to get my water from the pump below.

The mirror will reveal brown eyes full of intelligence and a capacity for pain; tongue, in all probability whitish, as it so often is nowadays. (My diet is bad, Excellency.) Stubble, evident but not too disfiguring—I go only twice a week to the barber. A used shirt, unfortunately. Tomorrow Kyria Antigone brings the washing. White linen trousers. One leg has got shorter than the other, over the years, owing to an uneven rate of shrinkage, but they are clean. Fingernails. A wet comb through the hair. No socks, which is a pity. I will discard my slippers in favor of the white and tan shoes. They pinch, but one must make some sacrifices. I go out three or four evenings a week, Excellency, normally: for information and—lower in the scale of things, but vital for continuance—food. Not the fez this evening, the straw hat. It will be obvious that I am not wearing socks, but no matter—my acceptance among the foreign community here is due largely to the fact that I provoke mirth and contempt in them. They see only an obese Levantine, scrounger and clown, one trouser leg shorter than the other.

Such judgments are irrelevant, of course, and yet they are what most people proceed on. Anyone coming in just before, for example, while I was sleeping, would have missed the fire and fever of my eyes, seen only the uneasy bulk, the sleep-dewed brow. Not that anyone could obtain entry. Not without a good deal of force and noise. My room is securely locked at all times. But of course they will, they will break in, sooner or later. It is only to be expected.

Broken man on the rough cross. Not much blood. His head was down, but he was still breathing. I saw the movements of his chest.

I was not surprised, Excellency. I was frightened by his face, but not surprised. I must start getting ready to go out.

Some minutes after midnight—I hear the first whistles of the night watchmen.

My room was as I had left it. Thankfully I slipped the shoes off my tormented feet. I stood for some moments in the darkness at my window, looking out. Faint glimmer of moonlight, starlight, on the sea. No lights along the shore. Plaintive whistle of the watchman, then again silence.

I am at my table. Thick felt across the window—it is unwise to show light when every man of worth, Muslim or *rayah*, should be sleeping. I am too excited to sleep.

Light from the spirit lamp falls on my pages. I love the look of paper in lamplight, the soft bloom on the loosely gathered pages. Around this charmed space the room falls away into obscurity. Here is *luxe, calme et volupté*. Here is where freedom and authority, spirit and form, embrace.

How shall I begin? Not, certainly, with the bald recital of my finds among Mister Bowles's luggage. That will have to be led up to.

The streets were dark, the only light coming from windows and the doorways of shops. We have no street lamps on the island, though there is a rumor that this year they will be installed—by an Italian company, who will certainly have offered large bribes to the appropriate officials. Forgive me, Excellency, if I speak disparagingly of your civil servants. But they are the most corrupt that the world has ever seen.

I went up by the steps. (There is also a road which climbs more gradually up toward the *plateia*.) I could hear the distant lamentations of the herded sheep. Pausing outside the magistrate's to get my breath, I breathed scented air from his garden, gulps of jasmine and mint. His shutters were not closed. I saw two men in the room overlooking the steps, neither of them known to me. Out at sea fishing lanterns in a looped chain.

Yannis was standing outside the hotel. He barely returned my greeting, but then he is always morose. I passed through the swinging doors into the lobby, saw Mardosian at the reception desk looking, as always, sleek and slightly troubled as if engaged in not quite satisfactory self-communings.

Excellency, that I have just mentioned these two men so scantly, in such summary phrases, as if they did not exist until my words called them forth, fills me with disquiet. They do exist. I cannot give equal space to all in one single report. Yannis from the Smyrna dockside, Mardosian who escaped clubbing in the massacres of the nineties to prosper here—they are mysteries, irreducible mysteries. Yet over the years, by constant reference, I have reduced them to my creatures, my props, just as I have made this island my territory. I swear I will not do this with Mister Bowles. I will render him direct, with sympathy and fidelity. I will seek to understand him, but will not fall into the error of regarding him as *transparent*.

I must admit that, as far as my personal relationship with him is concerned, I have not made a very good beginning. Things went wrong from the start.

I went on through the lounge, making my portly decorous way through the pink rattan tables and chairs. Following now the route which I had earlier imagined for Mister Bowles. On the walls familiar frescoes of the amorous metamorphoses of Zeus, executed by a German artist in the early years of the last century, crowded with bulky, frantic nymphs.

Across the carpeted floor, through the pillars and the potted palms, among which I suddenly saw old Mrs. Socratous, sitting reading the *Figaro Littéraire*. Or holding it, at least. Others there were too, islanded amidst the plants and pillars with the sound of music coming through to them from the dining room. Old people, for the most part, sitting very still. They were sitting very still, Excellency. Age and stillness combined at this moment to make them seem emblematic to me. I loitered for a while among the pillars, formulating sentences which might or might not go into this report. The good informer sees parallels everywhere, and this careful immobility reminded me of the state of the Empire. These people are dying, as we all are, as is the Ottoman power. They know it intimately, and seek by reducing movement to postpone the final pang, to achieve a sort of protracted moribundity. The lesson is plain: avoid sudden movements, Excellency.

Mrs. Socratous looked up with a brief glint through narrow, gold-rimmed glasses. Her fingers, much beringed, clutched the edges of *Figaro* with tenacity, as if there were much needed nourishment within the spread of the page. High on the wall beyond her, Zeus, in the shape of a white bull, was bearing off a massive-thighed Europa in dishabille. Mrs. Socratous did not smile exactly, but her mouth appeared to relax. I said, "*Kali spera sas*," and heard no response.

I passed on, entered the dining room and made my way directly across to the verandah at the far end. This verandah is long and narrow, with room only for a double line of tables. It has leaded glass panes on its outer side, and an elaborate framework of wrought iron, in the English style. Presumably used as a conservatory when the house was in private hands. (It was throughout most of the last century in the possession of the Zotas family.) Converted to its present use by the enterprising Mardosian.

The Englishman was sitting at one of the farther tables, alone. Exactly as I had envisaged! Indeed, as I look back on it now, this triumph, this exact coincidence with my expectation, acted like a spur to me, impelling me forward, arranging my face already into a smile. There were others on the verandah, Greeks of the town; among them was Politis the cotton merchant, with two younger men, one of them the brother of the priest, Spyromidis. At another table two Turkish officers from the garrison, in uniform. I was hardly aware of it at the time, being so intent on my meeting with the Englishman, but I seem to remember now that Politis did not return my greeting, and that the whole group was silent as I passed. I am almost sure this is so.

The Englishman looked up as I approached, glanced aside briefly, then regarded me steadily. I came to a halt at his table, removing my hat. His face was very real to me in this crucial moment of introduction: the long jaw and the thick fair moustache, eyes pale, rather narrow, very direct.

I paused, rather too long. The truth is, Excellency, that I was momentarily disabled by what I can only call his intenser physical existence. My own—and this may seem laughable in view of my undoubted corpulence—my own existence is liable to become quite unreal to me, especially when a strange face is confronting mine. I don't know whether it was because of this, or because the hostility of the Greeks, though still not fully registered, had thrown me off balance, but I now, on a strange impulse, in full sight of Politis, made the Moslem salaam, raising my hand to forehead and lips. "*Selamin Aleyküm*," I said.

Consciousness of my folly was immediate, and I felt fear, though not of those watching. "Excuse me, sir," I said, in English. "Can I have a word with you?"

At once, even while he was making a gesture towards the chair opposite, even before I was seated, I knew that I had struck a false note: my loss of poise at that crucial moment had made my manner too ingratiating. The English despise a too-evident desire to please. I fancied that I saw something change in his face, and I was distressed, because I wanted him to like me, or at least to see my worth. However, I went on talking.

"My name is Pascali," I said. "Basil Pascali. You are newly arrived on the island, I believe. I thought since I speak English, you know, after a fashion, that you might need some help . . . the services of an interpreter or guide. If I can be of any assistance to you, I hope you will not hesitate to ask."

(Here I must issue a small caveat, Excellency. I am reproducing this conversation some hours after the event. My faculty of recall is good, and it has been trained over the years, through the exercise of my profession. All the same, total fidelity is impossible; there must be some degree of manipulation. Anyone who writes reports will know that in the matter of dialogue, as in sequences of action, naturalism must often be sacrificed for the sake of coherence. My aim, as always, is to convey the essence through the form.)

About my own feelings, of course, there can be no mistake. And I will admit to your Excellency that I felt a degree of self-contempt to hear my own voice, before too deferential, now become boastfully assertive. "I live here, in the town," I said. "I am a well-known figure on the island. Everybody knows me. Everybody knows Basil Pascali . . . To make your stay more enjoyable, you understand."

He looked at me for some moments without replying, as

25

if he was waiting for something more. Then he said, "That is very kind of you, Mister, er, Pascali. My name is Bowles. Anthony Bowles."

His first words to me. First example of an incongruity about him which I found from the very first disturbing: the contrast between the unrelaxed yet leisurely movements of his body, and the blurting habit of his speech, in which bunches of words come out like offerings, full of haste and sincerity.

"There is a lot to see here," I said. "The island has a very long history as I am sure you know. It was one of the earliest Greek settlements. After that layers and layers of peoples, cultures. But I am sure you know all this. We are naturally very proud . . ."

I was attempting, you will understand, by these indirect means, to elicit something of the purpose of his visit. As I have already said, I do not believe he is here as a tourist. There is something different in the quality of his attention. Difficult to define. He made no immediate response to my remarks, and daunted by the silence I found myself looking fixedly at the level of Vermouth in his glass. I became aware of my own dry, nervous mouth. I am very sensitive, though few know this, and this meeting was so important to me. So momentous. His arrival, my departure . . . With my passion for portents, Excellency, you will see . . . Besides, I had felt from the beginning there was something between us. His present silence, however, gave me no help.

"You are younger than I thought," I said. "I mean, at a distance—"

It seemed to me that at this point Mister Bowles raised the level of his eyes slightly, as if to study the top of my head.

"Yes," I said, "I myself . . . I am getting thin on top, as they say."

I smiled at him, too familiarly. My face felt stiff. "You too," I said. "Slightly. If you will forgive me. But in your case it is at the temples."

. In order to establish comradely feelings between us, I

now decided to tell Mister Bowles the old joke about bald-ness. A mistake, as it turned out. "The men of this region," I said, "the men of the Levant—and I count myself one of them though my mother was English, primarily—we tend to wear thin on the crown, whereas with you it is at the tem-ples. This corresponds to our respective sexual mores, or so they say."

"Oh, yes?" he said, but without answering smile.

It was too late to stop now. I attempted a humorous leer. "We go straight at it," I said. "Like bulls, you know. Vigor but no finesse. It is the crown that bears the brunt. Whereas you . . . a more lateral, perfidious approach."

I began to illustrate the difference with motions of my head, wretchedly aware that I was failing to amuse Mister Bowles. It was he who brought my cavortings to an end with the offer of a drink. "Folklore," I said, returning my poor head to a position of rest. "The simple beliefs of simple people."

"Would you care for a drink?" Mister Bowles said again.

I pretended to deliberate. I am practiced in the quiet dignity of acceptance. (I do not wish to interrupt my narra-tive at this point, above all with complaints, Excellency, but I am forced by my low rate of remuneration to depend on others for many of the little extras of life.)

"Thank you, yes," I said.

He clapped his hands for the waiter. (He has been in these parts long enough to have adopted that custom, at least.) Biron approached at once and I ordered aniseed brandy. "*Kai mezedakia*," I said, to remind Biron to bring the little dish of olives and feta and scraps of anchovy which by custom accompany this drink and which had been my main reason for ordering it. I could not at this stage be sure of anything else to eat that evening.

The terrace had filled up without my noticing, so intent had I been on Mister Bowles. Another Turkish officer had joined the two at the corner table. They were drinking *raki*. The group around Politis was enlarged. Old Andrea was up on the little dais in the dining room with his violin, playing tunes from Offenbach and Strauss. The officers I had not seen before. Presumably new arrivals. The garrison has been strengthened since the attacks on Turkish detachments began. It is only two weeks since a platoon was ambushed on mountain patrol, and seven killed, including the lieutenant. The number of the rebels increases daily. They receive support from the villages in the interior. The people identify with them, co-religionists, fellow-countrymen.

Mister Bowles asked me how I knew English so well, since I was not English. He had not been listening then, completely. Perhaps a habit of his. Or did he wish to trap me in some inconsistency? I told him, which is true, about my lifelong admiration for the English language, its wealth and resourcefulness; about the English books in my house, which I have read so carefully, the Authorized Version, and *The Mill on the Floss* and the poems of Walter Savage Landor. Moreover, I reminded him, my mother was English. Primarily. I became too voluble, Excellency. I had drunk the spirits quickly, on a stomach virtually empty, and moreover I was feeling what I can only describe as a sort of wounded recklessness. I knew that I had failed to make the desired impression on Mister Bowles; I knew that he despised me; and with the perversity born of my hurt, I was disposed to play up to his contempt, to be the buffoon he had set me down for.

"Irish on her mother's side," I said. "She came out to Constantinople as a dancer and acrobat with a traveling show."

"Acrobat?" Mister Bowles seemed solemnly surprised at this.

"The two were quite often combined in those days. Cabaret artiste was a less respected profession than it became afterward. I don't mean *sexual* acrobatics. For that you had to go to the Armenian quarter." I paused to eat the last bit of cucumber on my plate. "Astounding agility those girls had," I said. "They would take on all comers. Ha, ha, forgive the pun. Including mules. Even now, if you know where to go . . ."

Mister Bowles nodded, and actually smiled at last, though as if humoring me. He showed no sign of wanting to follow up this topic. A pity, as I might have made a small commission.

"No," I said, "my mother simply varied her dancing with somersaults. I am talking about the eighteen-sixties now. All this was before the great days of the music hall, before June Avril and La Goulue."

I was beginning to blame Mister Bowles for his failure to see the rare spirit behind my possibly unprepossessing exterior. Already something unaccommodating, and perhaps even self-righteous, about him was making itself felt. All the same, as before, and despite myself now, I was constrained to his version of things, saw the gesturing, wheedling person he thought he was seeing. My self-demeaning was a game, a counterattack, but without hope of victory.

"Do you remember," I plowed odiously on, "do you remember that marvelous phrase Mallarmé used about Loie Fuller?"

"No, I don't believe I do," he said. "What was it?"

"*Fontaine intarrisable d'elle-même.*" I pronounced the French sonorously.

"Ah, yes," he said. "Would you like another drink?"

"That is very kind of you." This offer was humiliating, of course, as were the words I used in accepting it. I should have been less grateful, more *insolent*. (I have stores of insolence, Excellency; it is always the resource of the weak.) But the fact is that I had instantly become suspicious of him: it is not customary for bored, uncomprehending strangers to offer one second drinks—unless they are guided by self-interest. I wondered for a moment whether he simply wanted to shut me up. In that he would not have succeeded: I was about to introduce the Goncourts into our discussion of the music hall. But no. After another moment he leaned forward and said, in a burst, "That offer of yours, to act as interpreter, you know. Very decent of you. I may well take you up on it."

"At your service," I said.

"I have a spot of business to conduct here," Mister

Bowles said. "It's a question of making an approach to the authorities."

I think he would have said more, but at this point Biron returned with the drinks, and a moment afterwards Lydia Neuman appeared at the entrance to the verandah, and glanced round as if looking for someone. Presumably not seeing this person, she was turning back toward the door in the leisurely, indifferent way she has when she is alone and feels eyes upon her—I know her so well, Excellency. I wonder if I am the only one to find this assumption of indifference pitiful. Like all attempts to conceal vulnerability. On an impulse I waved and called her name. My voice caused a hush among those around Politis. Lydia saw me, hesitated briefly, then began to walk toward us. On her face the familiar, curving, faintly derisive smile.

Lydia lives on the island, Excellency. Part of the time at least. She has a house with a studio in the Turkish quarter. She is of Jewish extraction. The family is Spanish in origin, but her parents now live in France, in Lyon. Her father is a financier of some kind, quite rich. No political affiliations that I can discover. She herself is an artist. She paints the landscapes and people of the island.

We stood up as she drew near the table. I was beginning to make the introduction, but Mister Bowles forestalled me. "Bowles," he said, "Anthony Bowles." He stood very tall and straight, looking at Lydia unwaveringly.

I wonder now why he was so precipitate. Not shyness, surely? Was there some design in it? Was he wanting to make it clear that he and Lydia had never met before? The only reason for wanting to make this clear is that they have. Probably I am being too ingenious.

"Lydia is an artist, a painter," I said. I watched her slim, honey-colored hand enclosed in his reddish big-knuckled one, and a slight chill, a feeling of premonition, visited me at this brief engulfment. (As you know by now, Excellency, I am a believer in signs and portents. The world of sense signals to us, but all messages are encoded. The true *frisson* is in perception of the pattern, the overall design, not in the detail, however glowing. It is the same with a well-constructed report.)

"Mr. er, Pascali was just telling me about his mother," Mister Bowles said, when we were again seated.

"One of his favorite topics." Lydia smiled at Mister Bowles, establishing an immediate *front* with him against me. She is swift and always unerring in this forming of alliances—when she is interested in someone. Always this eagerness, this optimism, at every new acquaintance. Me of course she has placed and fixed, long ago. She knows my devotion.

I looked at her face in half profile, at the dark, strongly marked brows, dark eyes, high cheek bones, giving an effect of severity in repose—a severity cancelled at every slightest tendency of the mouth to smile. She was wearing a pale green crêpe dress embroidered with white braid at the throat. To my exacting eye the material seemed too soft and clinging for the spare lines of her body, the angular shoulders, the high breasts. I know her body in every detail, Excellency, though I have never seen it with the eyes of sense. Years of lonely fevers in my room, shuddering knowledge. She and I have done everything together.

"He likes to give himself disgraceful antecedents," she said.

Her own, apart from the bare summary I have given you, are shrouded in mystery. She was born in Vienna, she once told me, and was for some years at school in England, a boarding school in Kent. She speaks English well, though with a French accent. She makes fairly frequent trips to Europe. What she does there, I don't know. There is much I do not know about Lydia, even after so long, but one thing is certain: she enjoys powerful protection. An unveiled, foreign woman, living alone, coming and going as she pleases, she is nevertheless treated with deference. When she is away from home, a *bekirji* is more or less constantly stationed opposite her house during the nighttime hours. Whether she has friends at court or friends here I'm not sure—she does not see many people here; but friends she has, most assuredly. To take one privilege among many, small, but enviable, she is allowed to bring foreign books back from Europe without the zealous attentions of your Excellency's customs officials. More important, her journeys include visits to Athens and various parts of mainland Greece—this with the full knowledge of local officials here. However, I do not want to give the wrong impression. She is an accomplished painter, and takes her work seriously.

"His mother was an acrobat," Mister Bowles said. This fact seemed to have lodged firmly in his mind.

"Acrobat?" Lydia said. "He told me she was a piano-teacher."

Both of them turned to regard me with the same faintly derisive expectancy. I see myself as they must have seen me: obese, quaintly dressed, in manner and gesture effusive, face slightly moist from the exertions of speech; a man who accepts drinks and gibes, without reciprocating.

"My mother," I said, "belonged to a more innocent age than ours. The road show she was with fell on evil days. She took up the profession of prostitution in Constantinople, which in those days had nothing but very *fat* whores. Fatness was regarded as the sine qua non; there was no making a career without it. That is, until my mother appeared on the scene. Being in good hard training from her acrobatics, and with no superfluous flesh on her, she appealed to a special taste—one which up to then had been completely uncatered for. As you can imagine, she began to prosper.

"Of one of the encounters of those early days I am the unathletic product. I have no idea who my father was—begetter seems a more suitable word—what the race or background. My mother gave me different accounts at different times—she was a great one for stories."

"You have inherited that from her, at least," Lydia said.

Mister Bowles looked worried. "I don't really think—" he began, then stopped, aiming at me the reproof of his pale eyes.

"Yes," I said, "sometimes it was a person highly placed, sometimes a poor artist, sometimes a simple peasant. There

32

were times when I thought the whole race of men had gone into the making of me. Eventually, and to cut a long story short, my mother became the mistress of an official in the Ministry of Finance, a Maltese, by name Pascali. Through all these vicissitudes she kept me by her side. I learned English at her knee, Greek from tutors, Turkish on the streets, and French at the Lycée. But English, as I was telling Mister Bowles before you came, was always my favorite."

"A man's mother should be sacred," Mister Bowles said.

Lydia was gazing at him with interest. "Are you staying here long?" she said.

"Possibly a week or two. The whole area is rich in historical remains."

"Are you an archeologist, then?"

"Strictly an amateur," he said. "It is a hobby of mine and I can afford to indulge it. At present I'm gathering material for a book about the classical antiquities on the coast of Asia Minor and here, on the islands."

"There is a lot here that has never been touched," Lydia said.

"I am looking forward to investigating it." Mister Bowles leaned forward and looked intently at Lydia. He paused, as if gathering himself, and then the words came out in a rush: "The first settlers from Attica built a temple to Artemis up there, on the headland," he said. "But it seems that the area was regarded as sacred before that. Long before." There was a note of deep seriousness in his voice.

"Perhaps because there is water there?" I suggested. "Wells and watercourses have always bred superstitions, even faster than microbes."

I spoke in this disrespectful way deliberately to counteract what I felt to be the religiosity of his tone. However, he made no reply. He was still looking at Lydia. "Mister Pascali mentioned that you are a painter," he said.

"Yes."

"What kind of pictures do you paint?"

"Well," Lydia said, "landscapes mainly. With figures, you know. Though lately I have been doing some portraits."

She was settling down to tell him about her work. Suddenly I had an idea. With Lydia on this subject, neither of them was likely to move for quite some time.

"I'll be back in a minute," I said. Neither of them as much as glanced up.

Back through the palms and the pillars of the lounge, deserted now. The sense of being about to proceed illegally quickened my heart. I am a law-abiding man, Excellency. As I had expected, there was no one at all in the lobby, no one at the reception desk. Mardosian was making himself pleasant in the dining room.

Passing around the desk to the panel where the heavy brass keys hang on their pegs, actually reaching out and grasping number sixteen, brought me out in a general perspiration. Key in hand I went rapidly back around the counter, wheeled left up the stairs, slipped along the corridor to room sixteen. I opened and entered, breathing heavily with the exertions of my haste. The room was warm, shuttered. I saw at once that the Englishman had not yet fully unpacked. Both of his valises were on the floor between the bed and the wall. One was still locked, the other open and half-empty.

In haste I opened it wider, saw the folded clothing. I thrust my hand into the depths of it, working the palm against the inner cover, all the way round. I trembled with fear, but I persisted. (Excellency, I ask you to notice my dedication—greater because I am not naturally endowed with courage. Men are unequal in this respect, as in all others. This of course you already know. My poor store of knowledge is contained in one small corner of your spacious mind. However, I presume to remind you. Recesses in such vast estates may become shadowy. Even the mind of God, they say, is not uniformly lit.)

Two silk shirts with the label of a tailor in Pera. So he has been in Stamboul. Then, amidst yielding of cotton, my hand touched something cold, smooth, resistant. I drew out, drew up like treasure a smallish marble head of a woman. About as large as a man's fist. White marble, Paros

34

marble by the look of it, warmed with age. Stylized hair, broad Asian brows, blind smile. Nose rather badly chipped. Why is he carrying her about in his luggage? Perhaps acquired on his recent travels.

Nothing further of interest in the luggage. Though by now intensely desirous of leaving, I steadied myself, controlled my breathing. I began to go through the chest of drawers in the corner. In the second one I found a notebook with glazed black covers. The journal? However, all I could make out on the pages I hastily glanced at were figures and dates in red ink, some place-names, details apparently of expenditures in Turkish liras. My eye was caught briefly by an entry against Miletus, with figures in brackets. No personal opinions or impressions whatever.

With a sort of trembling tenacity of purpose I opened drawer after drawer; in the bottom one I was rewarded. There, quite alone, lay a short-barreled revolver with a black rubber grip. Squat and naked it lay there, no holster, no masking cloth. A dull shine to it, blue-black. I did not touch it, Excellency. I have a horror of firearms.

Here was a discovery indeed. Do amateur archeologists normally include instruments of death in their equipment? I think not. Strangely enough I no longer felt any fear: fear had been stilled by the sight of the weapon, as by a blow. I remained for a second or two longer in the quiet room. In my mind a vague sense that something had been confirmed. Then I withdrew quietly, passed back along the corridor, down to the lobby. Someone had been at the counter while I was upstairs, because there was an open copy of *Cumhuriet* on it. However, I am sure no one saw me replace the Englishman's key. Pausing only to wipe palms and neck with my handkerchief, I made my way back toward the verandah, catching as I did so the stern eye of the divine rapist, now in human form, in a blue cloak and spiked helmet.

"We're having dinner here," Lydia said. "Come and join us."

Thus assuring, bless her, my food for the evening. They

had been joined by Herr Gesing, the German commercial agent. He has not featured in my reports before, having only been on the island a week or so. . . .

I am very tired, Excellency. I cannot finish my account of the evening at this one sitting. I must postpone the rest until later today. My eyes ache, and the effort of focusing has become painful. Just now I opened the shutters a little and I saw light on the sea, the faintest swathe of light. Dawn has overtaken my labors. The sea lightens before the sky does at this time of year: a kind of luminosity on the face of the water, as if daybreak is more promptly and sensitively recorded there. This band of light extends as I watch, with the effect of a long slow ripple, like a tremor in a dream—neither pleasurable nor painful, but constrained, under duress. As always, I am impressed by the docility of the sea. It quivers to light and current like a vast belly twitching in a dream. . . . The sky above the hills lightens from minute to minute. Somewhere in the interior, beyond the bay, I see the smoke of fires. Lately I have seen them frequently, though not usually so near the coast. The smoke rises straight up in thin columns. Signals, cooking fires, it is impossible to tell. Too much smoke for shepherds' fires.

Before long the *imam* will be calling, reminding us that it is better to pray than sleep. I shall eat the olives and bread and salami which I managed to abstract from last night's supper (wrapping them in my napkin under cover of the table). While I am eating, I shall watch the distances of the sea define themselves, and the islands take shape—a process which never fails to please me, Excellency, giving me the same feeling art gives, that this could assume no other form, happen no other way. Then I shall sleep (behind locked doors), and afterward continue my report. I must omit nothing. Events must be dealt with as they occur. Otherwise I shall fall behind, and then death will overtake me, like this dawn, with something possibly vital, possibly the vital clue, left unrecorded. I cannot allow this to happen. I will not leave this room, I will not expose myself to new experience, until I have completed my account of last night. When they come for me everything will be up to date, up to the minute.

I HAVE JUST seen him, Excellency. Almost immediately after waking. I was sitting here at the window but had not resumed writing. He came down from the far end of the bay toward me, walking along the shore, near the sea. He passed below me and on past the café, where I could no longer follow him. Sand-colored shirt with short sleeves, trousers darker. Sun-reddened arms. Brown hat with a soft brim, pulled low over his eyes against the sun. He walked steadily, head up, swinging his arms very slightly. Where has he been at this hour? A morning stroll along the shore? There is something intent, fanatical almost, about the way he walks.

Why does he want my services as an interpreter? He referred to this a second time, while we were having dinner. Again, however, vaguely. "We must have a chat some time," he said. "You were kind enough to offer . . . My Turkish is not really up to it, you know, and when one is dealing with the authorities . . ." His eyes looking meanwhile at some point beyond me—presumably where his own purposes were visible to him.

This was later, in the midst of an argument with Herr Gesing, the German commercial agent. At first, for the first few minutes after rejoining them, I was so possessed by the strangeness of the objects I had found in Mister Bowles's room that I did not register what was being said around me. That strangeness possesses me again now. Revolver, head, notebook: violence, beauty, the meticulous recording of obscure facts. Forgive me for thus crudely drawing your attention to symbolic parallels, but you will see how once again this combination identifies me with Mister Bowles, links us together. As yet I cannot understand this, but persistence and cunning will make it clear—if I live, and continue to enjoy your patience, Excellency.

"Come on, Basil, tell us, why aren't you wearing your fez this evening?"

This is Lydia speaking to me now, in a slightly malicious, teasing voice. She wants me to sing for my supper.

"Surely one is allowed a fetish or two?" I look round the table, smiling. The fact is I have worn a fez on one or two occasions lately. Obeying a certain compulsion, Excellency. I found it years ago, in the Turkish quarter. It was early in the morning, I had been writing most of the night. There it was lying against the wall. Almost new. I tried it on —it fit me perfectly. I took it home with me. That was five years ago. Now, during these last few weeks, I have felt compelled to wear it from time to time. Dignified headgear, but hated by the Greeks, of course. "If we cannot have a fetish or two, where is liberty to be found?" I said, smiling at Herr Gesing, who did not smile back.

More than ever this evening Herr Gesing looked like a dropsical hawk, with his thin aquiline nose, full cheeks, small, heavy-lidded eyes, and above all the shape of his head, which is broad, and quite flat behind, falling almost sheer from crown to nape.

Lydia spoke softly to Mister Bowles, and they smiled at each other. Evidently getting on very well. I was briefly visited by the suspicion—occupational I suppose—that this particular gathering, though apparently fortuitous, had been long-planned. Mister Bowles with the glamour of the new-comer still on him, the glamour of someone who may be bringing changes, as Dionysus did to the people of Thebes; Lydia with her trips to Europe, her knowledge of the latest thing, her money—which does not, I think, come from selling paintings; Gesing and his undefined commercial activities.

I ordered *uvetzaki* and felt my mouth beginning to fill with saliva.

"How is trade?" I asked the German.

He looked up from his plate of fried squid and raised his thick eyebrows with an effect, quite accidental, of benevolence.

"The possibilities," he said, in his halting English, "the possibilities we are still . . . exploring. Exploring, *ja.*" His voice has a purring note, made from deep in the throat. He looked at our faces for a moment or two. "In the meantime," he said, "I enjoy this beautiful island, and the light, this unique light which so many sensitive observers . . . Of Goethe and Wincklemann I think now, among many—"

"Many lesser lights," I said. No one seemed amused by this.

" 'Who lives in this light, lives truly.' " Herr Gesing said. "Hugo Von Hofmannsthal it was, who said that. To nurse illusions in this clarity of the light, it is not possible."

All Germans, you will notice, Excellency. All the people he mentioned were Germans. This Teutonic blandness annoyed me slightly. I saw a chance to provoke some less guarded speaking, also to interrupt the cultural flow.

"It was a compatriot of yours," I said, "Gerhart Hauptmann actually, who was attacking the Greek spirit not very long ago. He was quoted in the *Mercure* as saying that the Greek tradition was anaemic. That was his word. He said it needs new blood. New blood. That was his phrase."

I saw the Englishman look up suddenly at Herr Gesing.

"Perhaps he meant German blood," I said, taking care, however, to preserve a smiling face. My *uvetzaki* arrived at this point, and I began on it at once.

"It is not typical," Herr Gesing said, with no change in his manner. "We Germans see in this landscape light as an expression of *Geist*—"

"Spirit," I said.

"Spirit, *ja.* Spirit and light together . . . *zusammen verbunden.*" He brought his hands together slowly and linked the fingers. "So," he said. "Many have spoken of this. . . . Rilke, it is Rilke who makes Apollo high among the gods, the god whose whole being in light finds expression."

"That's all very well," Mister Bowles said. "But what are you really after here?" He spoke in his usual blurting voice, as if speech came as a release from some tension or struggle.

"After?" the German said.

There was a silence, rather embarrassing. Naturally, we have all wondered. I have tried on several occasions, by discreet questioning, to find out from Izzet Effendi, the Pasha's land agent, what game the German is playing, whether he has some special influence locally. But so far without success. It is certain that he is on some sort of terms with the Pasha. He goes there, to the house. No doubt you will have had the police reports.

Herr Gesing had continued eating, moving his jaws slowly. Mister Bowles showed no sign of embarrassment. His eyes rested steadily on the German.

"After?" Herr Gesing said again. He had not understood the question. I feel it to be characteristic of Mister Bowles, even on this short acquaintance with him, that he should have been so blunt and idiomatic, making no concessions to the foreigner. (English prepositional usage is a great stumbling block, Excellency. I myself get it wrong sometimes.)

Hastily I swallowed my mouthful of mutton. "He means," I said, "what particular openings or opportunities are you looking for, here on our beautiful island?"

Herr Gesing raised his eyebrows. "The general possibilities," he said, slowly and carefully, "we are at present . . ."

"Exploring?" I suggested.

"Exploring, yes."

"I'll tell you what I think, old boy," Mister Bowles said. "Germany should make it absolutely clear where she stands on the question of the minorities before she looks for trade here, or anywhere else in the Empire."

The German raised the empty wine bottle. "*Bitte*," he called to Biron. "*Mehr Wein*."

"The Kaiser must be well aware of what is happening to the Christian minorities," Mister Bowles said. "Just as much aware as the Porte is."

"This is politics," Herr Gesing said. He wiped his mouth and repeated more loudly, "Politics."

I glanced around. No one seemed to be taking any particular interest in our conversation. Still, one has to be careful. There are spies and informers everywhere nowadays.

"You turn a blind eye to it," Mister Bowles said.

"Blind eye?"

"He means that you ignore it," I said.

"Trade we are interested in," Herr Gesing said. "Trade. And culture. Politics, no."

"Out of your own mouth." Mister Bowles nodded his head in solemn triumph.

"*Was meinen Sie?*"

"You keep them separate, those two? Politics and trade."

"*Natürlich.*" Herr Gesing looked round the table, spreading his hands. "They are separate things, *nicht wahr?*"

"That is the big difference between our two countries," Mister Bowles said. "Our policy, British policy, is shaped by ideals. We protested at the Armenian massacres, for instance. We lost trade as a result, of course. Germany said nothing. In fact, at the height of the atrocities, your Kaiser sent the Sultan an intimate birthday present, a signed photograph of himself."

I wonder how you felt on receiving that, Excellency? Typical piece of narcissism. Still it is true that since then Germany has lined her pockets in the Near East. You will have noticed that Mister Bowles, just as earlier in his comment about motherhood, had taken up a strongly moral position. However, he seemed sincere enough. Difficult not to admire his *saeva indignatio.*

"As a result, Germany got the Baghdad Railway concession," he said.

Herr Gesing was smiling. "Ideals?" he said. "It was not about the massacres the English were protesting. It was the loss of the eight percent from the Ottoman Loan Company."

"Nonsense," Mister Bowles said. He was looking flushed.

"Listen, to me. You must these moral categories transcend. We are moving toward the coming age. Like a great music. Like a symphony. You must hear all the music together. If not, you have only discords."

"Children bayoneted," Mister Bowles said heatedly.

"That is a discord."

"Women and girls raped and mutilated."

"On discord you are dwelling."

"Men with their testicles cut off and stuffed into their mouths."

"Discord, discord," Herr Gesing said.

I allowed my attention to drift somewhat. I felt comfortably replete. We were halfway through the third bottle of wine now—the lambent, amber wine of the island. However, in spite of this well-being, my mind began to fill slowly with thoughts of the bayoneted children, disemboweled before they could walk, the clubbed Armenians bleeding their lives away into gutters. All the rapes and mutilations and multilingual agonies of your possessions, Excellency. Together with the gratification they afford to the inflictors. Accents of pain and brutal jubilation, mingling and arising in one great vaporous exhalation. The world steams with it. . . . In Herr Gesing's discourse the wolf lies down with the sheep: Nietzsche red in tooth and claw, bedded with gentle Spinoza. Passing discord, ultimate harmony. "The knowledge of evil is an inadequate knowledge." God has no knowledge of evil. Those pleading in vain, the dispossessed, the violated . . . Even the crucified man with his half-open eyes and lolling discolored tongue. His misfortune is not that of the universe as a whole. . . . But it is, it is, Excellency. Harmonies are not composed in that way. Old friend Spinoza, why do I find your views, that have comforted me so long, so suddenly and so totally unacceptable? Can you not see the steam, Excellency, can you not see it from the windows of your palace? Perhaps not, perhaps you cannot see through your windows. . . . The steam condenses into blood.

"You are absolutely right. A country's foreign policy is the expression of its moral nature."

Lydia, saying things she does not really believe, in order to support Mister Bowles. With a kind of despair, remembered rather than felt, almost impersonal, like a summation of all my experience of loss, the rancidness of the detached observer, I take in the rich pallor of her face again, its severity mitigated, made strangely ambiguous by the heavy-lidded eyes, the curving smile. Her shoulders square, slight, under the clinging material of her dress, with its fashionable high neck. I summon to mind once again, with the patience of the habitual fantasist, her thirty-five-year-old body, naked as I have never seen it, luminous, lovingly supple. A body often petted and caressed, and the more precious for it, the more valuable for all that cherishing, those ardent traceries of hands and lips . . . For some reason, that smooth marble head in Mister Bowles's luggage comes into my mind.

"The values of that country registered in action. Like a work of art. A sculpture, for example."

It is all for him. The turns of her head, the movements of her arms, from which the wide sleeves fall away to reveal slender, pale-haired forearms. All for him. Gesing, I think, saw something of this: perhaps it was what had made him so inclined to argue. Mister Bowles himself appeared to notice nothing.

"Morality, religion, pah!" Herr Gesing said. He hit the table lightly with his fist. "Toward the realities we must look, and the future age," he said.

"Future age, eh?" Mister Bowles seemed somewhat dashed by this burst of rhetoric. He remained silent for some time. I heard Lydia ask the German what he meant by future age and I heard his reply, delivered with confident promptitude: "The coming age on nationalism will be founded. Nationalism, military organization, the competition of trade."

A good deal of discord there, by the sound of it. No mention of culture, either. Presumably Herr Gesing will divest himself of that in the lobby of the coming age. Lydia and Herr Gesing went on talking. I was about to break in to voice my horror, when Mister Bowles turned to me and in low tones once again spoke of the possibility of my acting as interpreter for him. But again in the vaguest terms.

"I am at your service," I said.

There was silence for a few moments. We all looked at Herr Gesing, who sat very upright in his chair, hands curled into loose fists resting on the table. Then Mister Bowles leaned forward and in tones of great seriousness, said, "If Germany puts self-interest before morality, she is heading straight for disaster, old man. No state can last long on that basis."

Herr Gesing regarded him in silence for a moment. His thin, scrupulously shaved lips formed slowly into a sort of pout, which managed to look judicious and derisive at the same time. "Every state behaves so," he said.

No one replied, and in the silence Herr Gesing stood up and took his leave, bowing first to Lydia and then, with an identical bow, to us. He made his way out of the verandah. He walks with strutting steps, holding his head well back on the short neck. There is something both absurd and impressive about Herr Gesing.

I myself left shortly afterward, weaving my portly and decorous way out, braving the glances from other tables. It was nearing midnight and I had my report to think of. I left the two of them there together.

It seems to me still, as it did at the time, that what Herr Gesing said about the behavior of states is true. Take only this matter of the treatment of Christian minorities in the Empire. Germany refrains from condemning the Porte, indeed she behaves as a friend, and so gains lucrative concessions in Asia Minor and permission to send German officers to train your army. All the other European powers condemn us, but none of them can agree to act because they are divided among themselves. Russia, still smarting from San Stefano, demands as a condition that the Straits should be opened to her ships of war. As neither Britain nor France will entertain this, Russia does nothing. France does nothing either, because she remembers 1870, and is unwilling to offend Germany. Moreover, she too seeks trade concessions in Anatolia. Britain will not act alone, preferring public expressions of outrage. (They call you "The Red Sultan," Excellency.) However, her main motive is not concern for the minorities, but fear of Russian influence in the Balkans. And her professions result in more suffering than would otherwise take place, since they encourage uprisings which have no hope of success, and which are put down with barbarous brutality by your Excellency's accomplished Cossacks.

In the web that holds all these powers together, morality is merely one strand, and that a weak one; at every intersection there is a *deal* of some sort, provisional and largely dishonest; gumming it all together a collective salivation of ambition and self-interest. (Some sentiment too, to make it sticky.) A very precarious web, Excellency. One shade the more, one ray the less, and the whole thing falls apart.

Once again I have allowed daylight to fade unnoticed while I sit here involved in my toil of words. Trying to get everything right. Beyond my window the glimmering sea and the first pale stars. Voices from the café along the shore carry faintly to me here. The lanterns have been lit on the café verandah. Their light falls across the shore to the water's edge. Shallow waves break into the light, seethe briefly, subside.

I remember the expression, the absence of expression on those faces in the hotel last night. Politis, the priest's brother, the other Greeks there. Not hostility, no longer hostility, but the stillness of a final judgment on those faces. None of them spoke. They know. Why have you left me alone here, among enemies, Excellency? Why have you abandoned me? I should at least have heard, like Antony, the music of departure. But there has always been silence. From the very beginning. You set me down here and left me. Or Mehmet Bey did so, on your behalf. The money every month through the Banque Ottomane, not increasing in spite of my many appeals, buying less and less, keeping me alive, after a fashion. No word of acknowledgment. No action ever taken as a result of my accusations, either of real

45

or imaginary persons. Is it to be wondered at that these latter came to preponderate? Is it so strange that I began to invent? Invention has been my chief delight, Excellency. This island and all the people on it are my inventions. I have even invented a persona for myself. But when these fictional persons come for me they will have real knives.

I kept no copies. At first I thought of it as too dangerous. And now that I have grown more careless of the danger, it is too late. I have no record of what I have written. All those words. The words falling, strewing the sheets, random as snow to my memory, falling and melting away behind me. Everything, in my devotion to duty, I sent to your officials. I have no means of recovering what I have experienced and known—except only by visiting the Imperial Archives in Constantinople, the rooms where the reports of spies are kept. Then I could see my work again, perhaps even make copies. I could edit and collate the material. Even, one day, I could publish, with suitable omissions and abridgments of course. A book, Excellency! What happiness that would give me. But to gain admittance, to obtain the necessary permits—a man as poor as I could not hope to do that.

Why have you abandoned me? I was twenty-five when I was recruited as one of your informers. Polyglot, literate, possessed of some charm of manner. A promising young man. I was established here on a rate of remuneration sufficient at that time for my needs. It was thought that I could watch the movement of ideas among the more educated on the island—the spread of nationalism among the subject peoples, constitutionalism among the Turks, the affiliations and activities of foreign visitors. This I have done—with the various imaginative additions freely confessed to. I have also watched men less endowed grow rich while I crouched here at my table, with my view of the sea, my view of the workings of people. None of this I would have minded, for I realized even in those early days, before my style had developed, that I had stumbled on my métier. I would not have minded, but for the silence, the absence of recognition.

I look around my room now, in the lamplight: the square table before me, the upright chair, pale lemon in color, on which I sit; the narrow bed against the wall and its faded quilt; my triple row of books, schemed for, stolen, bought with the scrapings of piastres—Sherlock Holmes, *Candide*, The Greek Testament, *In Memoriam*. Books, my consolation. My nargileh in the corner, given to me before his death by Ibrahim Turgut. On the narrow bench against the opposite wall, my spirit stove and coffee-making appurtenances—and my telescope, stolen from an Italian gentleman six years ago.

It is not much. Forty-five years I have been in the world. All those moments of perception and sensation, pulse beats of my life, reduced to this. I have no family, no children, no great possessions. A woman to cry for me, a *yali* on the Bosphoros, such things would at least be tangible evidence of a life. As it is, five minutes' work of clearance would remove forever all evidence of my existence. Other occupants there will be, knowing nothing of Basil Zavier Pascali. Nothing I see pleads for me, upholds me as a person, makes me feel more than a temporary vehicle for someone else. Perhaps you, Excellency? Your thoughts are crowded, so you need an annex. I do not think, I am thought with. *Ergo?* An illusion too this heavy flesh responding blindly to imperatives from elsewhere. I do not lust, I am lusted with. All illusion. Only the words as I write have a brief radiance of reality, for the moment only.

Taking into account that my earlier reports were much sketchier, and that I have increased steadily in output until now my activity is virtually incessant, I calculate that I have addressed well over a million words to your officials at the Ministry, and they have vanished as into some kind of mighty pit. The Imperial word-pit, specially limed to reduce all verbiage, however densely written, however solidly informative, to sludge.

No trace of those words, except the marks on my face that the struggles with them put there . . . I must stop now, Excellency, rest my eyes a little. Perhaps a stroll along the

47

shore. I am reluctant these days to go out, but this is a good moment. I am up to date with my report.

I DID NO MORE last night, Excellency. Now I am here again, at my accustomed place. Sky and sea empty. No sign today of the American's caïque. Shore empty too, except for the sardine fishermen, just beginning to haul in the nets. Seven men, possibly eight. At this distance merely a ragged horizontal mark, but human, violent. The sea tormented with light, assailed by glittering splinters. The whole bay quivers with brilliant pain.

Soon it will be time for Hassan, the shore fisherman, to emerge from the shadow of the café, step out onto the bright empty shore with his gathered net, like a person entering another's dream. Hassan and his net provide me with analogy, a high service. He was sent to me, I am convinced of it, sent to me at the beginning of my report, when I was passionately eager to write everything to you, Excellency, everything without reserve; he was sent to warn me against attempts at such inclusiveness. Picture the net at its moment of meeting the water. I mean, as thrown with all Hassan's cunning. It meets the water at fullest extent. That moment is the net's perfection of form—but it is a perfection defined by what it must necessarily *exclude*. Exactly that perfection is what I seek in this report. You see how it is, Excellency? We live in a world of mutually reinforcing images, and God pays me in insights for my attention to this world.

He has just appeared again, this time walking in the opposite direction, along the shore toward the headland. Not Hassan, the Englishman. Mister Bowles. I looked up from the page and saw him, midway between the water and the

48

wall. Dressed again for walking, in heavy shoes, loose-fitting gray trousers, the same brown hat. I watched his figure slowly receding against the coruscating expanse of the bay. When he was beginning to grow indistinct against the rocks of the headland, I went and got Signor Niccoli's telescope. Now I could see him clearly again, walking steadily, looking neither to right or left. I had assumed that when he reached the limit of the bay he would turn back. He could, of course, if he wanted to walk farther, clamber over the rocks and get down into the next, much smaller, bay—from that point to the head of the promontory there is a series of rocky inlets. However, he did neither of these things. When he was nearing the low wall of rock he turned away from the sea, crossed the upper, steeper part of the shore. He disappeared for a minute or two, then I saw him again higher up, watched him climb until he was lost among the rock and scrub of the foothills.

Where is he making for? Perhaps that fold in the hills, above the old harbor, the area he spoke of. Prosecuting his researches. Possibly. But there could be other reasons. He could be making his own survey of the coast—for landing stages perhaps, or seeking some contact with the people in the interior. There are, as we all know, rebel forces in the mountains. We see their fires. Your troops are ambushed in lonely places. These people come down into the villages for supplies and nobody says anything. It may be that Mister Bowles has come to give them encouragement or money, stir up a bit of murder—for the best of reasons, no doubt; reasons these days are always excellent. Deaths here could be of benefit somewhere, to someone, provide a bargaining point, strengthen an argument. The Powers dabble in blood, if you will forgive the play on words.

We must make no violent movements, Excellency. We must emulate Mrs. Socratous in the lobby of the Metropole, keeping as still as possible. Your Empire is the most cosmopolitan the world has ever seen, a multiplicity of races, creeds and tongues, united in the Ottoman state. A perfect equivalent, in political terms, of that unity in diversity which

49

has exercised philosophers ever since Thales. (He held the opinion, if you will remember, that the world, in spite of all appearances to the contrary, is made of water.)

This unity can only be preserved by our remaining immobile. Avoid sudden gestures, Excellency. Avoid detonations. Avoid radical reform. There are certain phases in the progress of decay which can become interminable. We are living through one such. They have called us the Sick Man of Europe, but invalids can outlive their squabbling heirs. Let us aim at protracted moribundity. Make repairs by all means. Soothe local discontents. Review the pay structure for those in government service, especially your faithful and anonymous army of spies. That much motion will serve to keep carrion birds at bay.

The particles cluster to you, their natural lode and only attractive principle. By granting constitutions you will break this field of force. And what will they do, with their shining new nationhood, the Serbs, Bulgarians, Albanians, Macedonians? I will tell you, Excellency. They will devise uniforms and anthems and distinctive ways of marching on parade. They will be quick to take offense. It is a dignified thing to be a nation, and honor can only be served by inflicting atrocities up and down your new-found borders. More important than this, there is the attitude of the Powers to be considered. Take Austria, for example. Italy could shut off the Adriatic tomorrow, if she wished. If that were to happen, think how important Salonika would become to the Hapsburgs. Do you think they will allow the Slavs autonomy in Macedonia?

It is more than thirty years since your accession, and I have seen your dominions loosening, falling away from year to year. You must keep still, Excellency.

Why is it that I feel uneasy, giving this excellent advice of a faithful servant? Perhaps I smell again that steam of your Empire, vaporized blood. It hangs in the air of our immobility.

What is he doing, up there in the hills? Lydia may know

something. A visit to her studio might elicit some information, or at least, though lower in the scale of things, food. I have not yet eaten today.

I DID NOT CONTINUE yesterday, feeling tired after my visit to Lydia's studio. Tired and unwell. In fact I almost lost consciousness, on the steps up to my balcony. That was after leaving the Englishman. The blood was beating in my head and my vision was impaired for some minutes. I went to bed but could not sleep for a long time, not till early morning. Today I feel better. I need new glasses, Excellency. These I have had for ten years now. I was giving French lessons during that period to the daughters of the magistrate and to the Assistant Chief of Police, and I was able to save a little. I got the glasses in Smyrna. They are good glasses, but my eyes need stronger lenses now.

I know what it is that Mister Bowles requires of me. He arrived at the studio not very long after I did. Doctor Hogan came too, a little later. Lydia was working when I arrived, but seemed not to mind being interrupted. We talked about Mister Bowles for a while, and then, after he arrived, about painting. This conversation afforded a number of insights, important, I think, in this narrative of mine. I shall describe it in more detail later, but I must speak first about Mister Bowles's proposition.

When I got up to go Mister Bowles offered to accompany me, rather to my surprise. He had been annoyed, I think, by some remarks of the doctor's, and I thought at first that he was leaving because of this, but it was not so: his real reason soon became plain.

We walked for some time in silence. It was mid-afternoon and the sun was high, though the house walls on the seaward, western side cast a narrow shadow. Our steps were quiet in the dust of the street. We passed one or two Moslem women, no men. They were quick to cover their faces, no doubt because of the tall fair foreigner walking beside me.

Mister Bowles began to speak about his archeological interests. He was particularly interested in the site of the sanctuary to Artemis and in the area adjoining this. "Up there in the hills, you know," he said, not looking at me—he did not look at me while he was speaking, and nothing could have made him seem so alien to the ways of the Levant. Still, for a dedicated informer what could be better than to see Mister Bowles unfolding his obsessions, watch the movements of moustache and pale lashes? "No one has ever really looked at it," he said. "There are some extensive ruins there. Also the remains of a villa of the early Roman type." He did look at me now, quickly, as if these last words were in some way revealing. After a moment, he said, "It is believed to be the house to which the Virgin Mary retired after the death of Christ."

"That is the local legend," I said.

But it was not merely local, it seemed. In a series of bursts Mister Bowles indicated that it was a belief of very respectable antiquity. There were references in contemporary authors, though admittedly not conclusive. "St. Jerome," he said, "speaks of an island in the Greek Sea as having been the last resting place of the Mother of Christ. And Thornton, the English traveler Thornton—"

"But by 'the Greek Sea,' he must have meant the Western Aegean, surely?" I said.

Mister Bowles went on as if I had not spoken, merely raising his voice a little. "The English traveler Thornton—" he repeated. It was as if he was reciting something, almost, and was dutifully determined to get through to the end. "He was here in 1703," he said, "and he refers to the belief, then generally prevalent, that this was where the Virgin spent her last years." People used to come from as far away as the mainland, apparently, to intercede at her shrine.

"The Greeks burn a candle up there sometimes," I said. "When they want to give thanks to the *Panagia* for some favor, a good olive crop or a male child, something like that."

Mister Bowles nodded at this, soberly, and said he would put it in his book. He was writing a book about the various places that claim sanctity on the grounds that Mary breathed her last there. "There are eight altogether," he said. "Shall we walk down to the shore?"

We were among the Greek houses again now. We turned down toward the sea. Pappoulis was standing at the door of his taverna, clicking his tongue at the caged goldfinch on the wall. He nodded to me, but said nothing, and after a moment looked away. He did not speak to me, Excellency! Only last week, only five days ago, we played chess together. Fear came like nausea to the pit of my stomach. Pappoulis was averting his eyes from my death. For a moment, there in the sunlit street, the crucified man of my memory swung and creaked in his ropes. *Mon bon cadavre, o ma mémoire.*

"Turks too," I said. "They go mainly for the spring water, which they regard as holy, possibly through the association with Mary, and therefore good for the bowels. Typical of Moslems to reverence the laxative in this way."

How naturally concealment comes to us, Excellency. Here I was, possessed by fear of death, talking thus lightly. The Englishman's face was placid. What fears was he concealing?

We walked down to the shore and sat on the low wall above the shingle. I removed my hat and wiped the perspiration from my brow. It was cooler here. We could see the whole sweep of the bay, out to the headland. Mister Bowles went on talking. There were five in Asia Minor, he said, two in the Greek Archipelago, one on the Black Sea coast. Again I had an impression of recital, of a lesson learned. The sites were diverse, the evidence in some cases scanty, but the common claim, he was hoping, would suffice to give unity and interest to his book. Had he published anything yet? I asked him. No, not yet. We have an aspiration in common then.

From here we could see something of the area he had spoken of. We could see at least part of the path of the spring. Even at this distance, even in the heat haze, the seam of green where the spring took its course was clearly visible, as were marks of human habitation amidst the shrub and granite of the slopes. A kind of dereliction existed there to be found only where there has been human order previously.

"What I want, you see, is to obtain some kind of lease. For a month, say. Then I could come and go as I please." He was still looking up toward that scarred bit of hillside. "I could conduct my researches freely," he said.

"The land," I said, "belongs to Mahmoud Pasha."

"Who is he?"

"He is the Commandant of the garrison. He is also *de facto* if not *de jure*, the Governor. He is nominally responsible to the *Vali* of the Eastern Isles, but Mytiline is far from here, and in any case the *Vali* is fully occupied with hashish and harem."

"Does that mean the land belongs to the state?"

"No, no, it is in the private possession of the Pasha."

It is possible that you already know this, Excellency, but Mahmoud Pasha has been acquiring all the land adjoining the coast on this side of the island. Or rather, Izzet Effendi, his jackal, has been acquiring it for him. Just why is not yet clear to me. The coastal strip itself is good land, but they have extended their operations up into the foothills. A number of families, Greeks mainly, but also some Bosnians, have been ousted more or less, poorly compensated. Virtually dispossessed. It is said that several of the men have gone to join the bandits in the interior. Men with a grievance are dangerous men, Excellency.

"This Mahmoud Pasha can be approached, I suppose?" Mister Bowles said.

54

I did not reply immediately. In fact, I could not see what he hoped to gain by applying for a lease. Unless, of course, he had motives other than the one he had declared to me.

"They would not allow you to remove anything," I said. "Not without a *firman*, and you would only get that from Constantinople."

"I realize that," he said, rather stiffly. "I have no intention of doing any digging."

"In that case, if you will excuse me, I see no point in the proceeding you have in mind. You already have what amounts to free access to the area. Your movements will have been noted already, and reported to the Pasha. There are spies everywhere these days. Since no attempt has been made to limit your movements, you have nothing to gain by applying for a lease."

He turned to me at last, looked at me fully, hesitated, plunged into speech. "Oh, I must have a lease, you know. I mean to say, it is the proper way to go about things. I wouldn't be happy if everything wasn't quite legal and aboveboard."

There was an immense sincerity in these simple words of Mister Bowles. Not only personal rectitude was contained in them, but an obvious belief in the legality and above-boardedness of the universe as a whole. He looked at me, and though I was not more than a meter away, I was not the center of his vision, but simply one element in this ordered universe. It was absurd, of course. For I had in my mind what Mister Bowles could not possibly have had in his, a picture of Mahmoud Pasha, and his land-agent, Izzet. Your official representatives, Excellency. The Pasha enormously fat, almost immobile, some clogging of breath in the depths of him, wheeze of depravity and avarice; Izzet delicate-boned, beaky, vigilant, like a well-groomed vulture. These two do not belong in Mister Bowles's universe of due form and procedure. They do not represent order. *Ordure*, more like it. I felt a strong desire to laugh.

"I think it's the best policy in the end," he said. "What

55

I was going to ask you is whether you would arrange things for me. And act as interpreter. My Turkish is nonexistent, I'm afraid. For a suitable fee, of course."

"Oh, no, no, no," I said.

"Yes," he said, "I must insist on that."

I did not protest any further. I am always in need of money, as you know, Excellency. Besides, I was curious. I promised to arrange an interview with the Pasha through Izzet, and after one or two expressions of appreciation on his part, and modest rejoinders on mine, we parted.

Now, however, back here at my table, shore and sky and sea outside at their usual conspiracies, that feeling of puzzlement returns to me. Some faint sense of discrepancy hangs over Mister Bowles, some failure in correspondence. Informers develop a fine sense for such things. When he asked me about Mahmoud Pasha, he did not seem interested greatly in my reply. It is true that there is a certain habit of nonchalance about him. Perhaps it was no more than that. And yet, I had the feeling I was confirming things for him rather than giving him information. Perhaps he has made preliminary inquiries elsewhere. Quite a sensible thing to do. But in that case why question me?

IN FULFILLMENT of my undertaking I went to see Izzet Effendi this morning. His office is on the second floor of his house, in Sardou Street. It was cool and latticed. Izzet was wearing a Western-style jacket too large for him and a fez. He looked even frailer and more feverish than usual, as if consumed by the heat of his greed. There was a picture on the wall of Your Excellency, on a white horse, as you were at your accession. What hopes we had of you then.

"You look ill," Izzet said. "Your color is not good."

I explained I had not been so well lately. We drank tea, chatted for some time. He treated me politely. Izzet knows everything that the Pasha knows, and a great deal more, but I do not get the impression that he knows what I am. However, it is possible that he does, and he is quite capable of the guile and patience not to use his knowledge till the moment comes.

After the period consistent with courtesy had passed, I broached the subject of Mister Bowles, and his desire for a lease. I had to choose my words carefully. In these days of dissolving loyalties and universal chicanery, with adventurers from all over the world thronging into your possessions for what they can pick up, your officials add to their normal dislike for foreigners an almost pathological suspiciousness, based on the fear that others, cleverer than they, may be quicker to see opportunities for plunder. With this in mind I portrayed Mister Bowles as rich, naively honest, eccentric—for otherwise why would he want to investigate ruins?—not overburdened with brains. The archetypal Englishman abroad, in fact.

I put a good deal into this portrait, stressing particularly the Englishman's readiness and ability to pay; and I am confident that I succeeded in arousing Izzet's interest. His face remained impassive, but I detected cupidity in the cordial pressure of his hand when I took my leave. Mister Bowles and I are to present ourselves at the Governor's house tomorrow morning at ten o'clock. This will give Izzet time to see his master and discuss the matter. I have left a note for Mister Bowles at the hotel, telling him of the arrangement and promising to call on him there half an hour beforehand. There seems little more, for the moment, that I can do.

I did not complete my account of the visit to Lydia's studio yesterday. Yesterday or the day before? My sense of time, of the sequence of days, is growing vaguer, spending as I do so much of my life enclosed here, writing all hours, eating and sleeping irregularly. It is afternoon now. Outside, the prolonged outcry of cicadas, buzz of summer. I cannot work on the balcony, it is too exposed. I am too vulnerable there to distraction and fear. So I sit here in pajamas, against the heat.

I remember the light. It was the time of day when light is fully revived, fully quickened, but mild still, blooming on the white walls of houses. (Our island houses are white for the most part, Excellency. Shallow roofs, railed balconies, heavy wooden shutters). I stood for some time at the upper end of Caritas Street looking down over the orange trees and the dome of the *cami* at a segment of sea with fishing caïques laid on it one behind the other, receding into the haze of distance. The nearest had a red hull. Flat, resinous gleam on the sea; the boats looked trapped in it, expiring with a faint tremor of sails. Not real movement, probably, but a trick of heat or light. There *is* no real movement.

From somewhere near at hand, somewhere above me, the soft, plaintive bleating of a sheep. I looked up but could not see it. The light hurt my eyes. Waiting on some balcony for the sacrificial knife. How far is it off now, the Sacrifice Festival? Three, four days. Caritas Street was like a tilted trough, brimming with light. Intermittent tic of shadow cast by the low-flying falcons. My steps were muffled in the dust. That solitary bleating started off others. From all around me, all down the street and the streets around, plaints of tethered sheep. Bought some days in advance when the prices are better, tethered to balcony rails or gateposts, they suffer in the heat. The individual sound is trivial, but there is terrible anguish in this sustained collective cry. It rains down on me like the light. Through this chorus, from a neighboring street I heard the jingle of harness, the creak of a burden.

Three people I passed on my way up this street, but spoke to none of them, fearing a rebuff or worse. I saw myself with their eyes: my obesity, crumpled suit, straw hat, monogrammed handkerchief cascading from pocket. They do not see my fear.

I have betrayed myself, Excellency, in a number of ways.

Neither deliberately nor involuntarily. It has happened as things happen in the constraint of dreams. I have consorted openly with Turkish functionaries. Sometimes I use Turkish forms of salutation, sometimes Greek. I go to the mosque, perform the gestures of prayer. I also attend church, where I do not forget to cross myself. I am now in religion as I have long been in sexual matters, *utriusque capax*. The Moslem prayer fascinates me, the gestures, hands and minds reaching toward the void. . . . I know why I have allowed myself to become suspect, put my life in danger. I have understood something, Excellency. Human beings prefer destruction to perfect balance. What is intolerable, more intolerable than anything atrocious that the mind can think, is equilibrium. Twenty years, my stipend arriving regularly through the Banque Ottomane, my reports going out month after month. No response, no reaction. You see? A closed circle. A continuous celebration. And in this clarity of the light, as Herr Gesing would say. Intolerable. You see, doubtless you see, why I had to break out. My way is to make myself a victim. Others will break out by seeking me. . . .

At the end of Caritas Street there is a small paved square with a *periptero* in the middle and a narrow border of hibiscus bushes on two sides. The far side faces Avenue Alexandras. I paused here, debating whether to buy cigarettes. I never spend even small sums without deliberation, especially at this time of the month, with my next remittance still some days away. As I was hesitating, a ragged squad of troops with a corporal at the head came marching along the avenue in the direction of the garrison barracks. They were marching at ease, rifles slung. Mongolian faces these, flat, big-boned, sullen with weariness. None of them glanced in my direction.

I bought the cigarettes. On the other side of the avenue is where the Turkish quarter begins. I met Zeki Bey, the *mudur* of the school. Like many teachers and intellectual persons, Zeki Bey is on the side of constitutional reform. As far as I have been able to discover, he has no direct associations with the Young Turk movement, but he is certainly sympathetic to some of their aims. (I once alleged to your officials at the Ministry that he was a Freemason, but he had beaten me at chess and I was piqued.) We talked mainly about the killing of the five Turkish soldiers in the ambush. I asked him if he thought the garrison had been strengthened, mentioning to him the troops I had just seen. He said that he thought this was probably the case, though he had seen no troops arrive. Probably they had disembarked at night. Zeki Bey gave it as his opinion that the rebels in the hills are being actively supported, with guns and money, by agents in the pay of Athens. He spoke as one with special knowledge, but everybody says the same thing. "This American," he said. "Why does he remain offshore so long?"

"Who, the sponge-fisher?"

Zeki Bey smiled slightly, as if he pitied me. An offensive smile, Excellency. "They have searched his boat," he said. "This morning."

"Who told you that?" I said, smiling in my turn, as if I did not believe it.

But Zeki has too much self-esteem to be drawn in that way. "I was told," he said, and stopped smiling. I judged it better not to pursue the matter. I do not know if they found anything, Excellency. Lydia thought not, when I spoke to her later at the studio.

I must break off for a while—my eyes are heavy. Late afternoon is not a good time for me. Night is the best time for composition.

LYDIA CAME to the door in response to my knock. She explained at once, though seemingly without displeasure, that she was working. I thought for a moment or two she was going to send me away. But she needed a break, she said, she had been working all morning. I followed her upstairs—the ground floor of the house is completely unoccupied. We went through the small living room into her studio. This was originally two rooms and is now one, running the whole width of the house, with a large square window at both ends. I am always slightly ill at ease in this room, self-conscious, because of the flooding amplitude of light and the clutter of objects.

In the center of the room she stopped and turned to face me. She was wearing a sort of turban, white in color, tied at the nape of the neck and covering her ears and hair completely, so that the face she presented to me was that of an acolyte of some kind, a naked, devotional oval, and this impression was strengthened by her devotee's long smock of coarse white muslin reaching midway down the calves. Her legs and feet bare. Narrow, beautiful feet. On the smock, on the right side, just below the ribs, a smudge of red paint. Just the one mark. She had wiped her hand there, presumably.

"You have lost weight," she said.

"Dieting," I said. I was so pleased that she had noticed me to this extent that I found her gaze difficult to support. I motioned toward the painting in progress, on the easel, and said something appreciative about it. I forget now what. It was nearly finished as far as I could judge—an island landscape with peasants and goats. It was good, in the way that Lydia's paintings are always good: classical in spirit, very exact in perspective, with a loving fidelity to the volume and texture of things—leaves, rocks, clouds. Also to the effects of light. This clarity of the light.

We talked about various island matters, and then about the world at large. I enjoy my talks with Lydia. She travels, always has news and gossip. She knows what is happening in Europe, the movements that are forming, the books that are being written. It was she who told me about Strindberg, whom I had never heard of before, after seeing one of his plays in Paris. She brought back a copy of Gorki's

Mother in French last year. Now she was telling me about a Spanish painter named Picasso, who I had heard of but knew nothing about, and a book called *Three Weeks* by an Englishwoman, which is a great success. Lydia exhibits her paintings in Europe, but I do not think she can live on this alone. Probably she has money from her family, or has some of her own. Perhaps she is in your pay, too, Excellency? From what she tells me, almost everyone in Constantinople is a spy now. She said you are no longer seen in public, that you remain always immured in your palace of Yildiz, that even for the Friday prayers you do not show your face to the people, but go to the mosque in a closed carriage. The story goes that you keep a revolver in every room for fear of attempts on your life, that you shot and killed one of your gardeners whom you met by chance in the grounds, mistaking him for an assassin. It is said you live in hourly fear, Excellency. How strange if this were true. The Commander of the Faithful, God's Vice-Regent on earth—subject to the same sweating intimations of dissolution as this your humble informer . . . But I will not believe it. You are my only recourse, Excellency, my only hope of justice against your officials at the Ministry. I must continue to believe in your authority and power. *Si Dieu n'existait pas . . .*

In order to change the subject, I asked Lydia what she thought about the American. Or rather, I first asked her if she had met him; and it was her way of answering this simple question that alerted me to something odd, a puzzling inconsistency, slight but definite. Simple questions often expose complex deceits.

"This Mister Smith," I said, "have you met him?"

"Yes," she said. "No, I haven't. I've heard of him."

Heard of him. Strange phrase, Excellency. And then the contradiction. As if, intent on an untruth, she had told the wrong one, then fallen into too great a frankness.

"I exchanged a few words with one of his crew," she said. "An Italian. Two or three days ago. He came ashore for provisions. An elderly man."

"I see," I said. "Do you think the sponge fishing is genuine?"

"Certainly."

"I mean, do you think that is all he is here for?"

"If they'd had any doubts," Lydia said, "they'd have boarded him and searched."

"Apparently that is just what they have done."

"What do you mean?" Lydia's voice had sharpened. It seemed to me that a slight flush had risen to her cheeks. I passed on Zeki Bey's information to her. She was silent for a few moments, then she said quietly, "What fools they are."

"How do you mean?"

"As if a man like Smith is going to be caught by a routine search."

Again this suggestion in her words of some further knowledge of the American. I did not understand her attitude, Excellency, but did not think it politic at that point to press the matter any further. Instead I adverted to the topic I knew would interest her most—knew it with pain and resignation.

"Naive of Mister Bowles," I said, "to expect states to behave morally. Don't you think so?"

"He has a very strong sense of responsibility," Lydia said. She was standing at the window which looked out over the interior courtyard of the house. "He is quite unsophisticated in some ways," she said. "Unsophisticated in the best sense, I mean. A moral primitive." She uttered this last phrase with a certain enthusiasm, as if it augured well for Mister Bowles's vigor and general prowess. She moved against the window and the light defined her form within the loose-fitting muslin gown.

I have been in Lydia's studio often, but the light always surprises me, its plenitude and impartiality. It floods through the windows at either end, and occupies the room totally: full, white, stark without bleakness. There is no eddying, as there might have been at street level, vagaries caused by stirred foliage, or passers-by, no flex or play of light whatever. Bodies become like other objects in this light, seem to lose autonomy. I had a momentary sense that Lydia and I were in danger of being fixed there forever, she at the window, with her naked, undefended face, I standing smiling awkwardly there; figures in an interior created by some much superior artist; fixed forever along with all the other objects disposed about the room, objects with nothing in common except their unalterable stillness in this light —lacquered boxes, the polished vertebrae of a goat, a stuffed oriole with beautiful amber eyes, cloth flowers under a glass dome, twisted shapes of wood, fragments of glass, shells, shards, heterogeneous scourings of the island. When I spoke again it was with the conscious intention of distinguishing myself from these objects.

"Why do you think he is here?" I said.

"He told us. Weren't you there? He is interested in the ruins up there, in classical antiquity generally. He's writing a book."

She made a vague gesture with her arm toward the ceiling, as if to indicate the hills where the Englishman's true interests lay. I was again aware of the red mark on her side, and the shape of her body inside the gown. A curious compound of regret and desire stirred in me, and something else I had never felt before, pity for Lydia and for her and my mortality. She has been the victim of my fantasies for many years, Excellency. Now here she was, robed and marked for someone else.

"There are whole areas of his past life that he seems to just wince away from," she said. "As if you had touched some wound."

Something almost fanatical in the face, when unsmiling. And framed by the headcloth . . . It is clear that he has inflamed her female intuitiveness, a more effective organ of stimulation than some more obvious ones that spring to mind. Whether by accident or design or, as I suspect, some blundering amalgam of the two, he has got himself cast as a Man of Sorrows. That seems to be the fashion for contemporary heroes. The sensual fires are stoked by guilt these days, not a common love for keyboard music. Mister Bowles has the right whiff of unhappiness about him, it seems. Taciturn, though vibrant-hearted. Lydia is proceeding from the evident taciturnity to the presumptive vibrancy. Doubtful logic. Pardon me, Excellency, it is my jealousy speaking. All the same, I was surprised to see Lydia, so experienced in love, making this leap of faith.

I found the notion of Mister Bowles wincing away from the past interesting on other grounds. There could be reasons for a man to be evasive about the past other than that he is consumed by a secret sorrow—he may be consumed by a strong desire to cover his traces, for example. And Mister Bowles has so far succeeded in fending Lydia off when she inquired about his past. No mean achievement when the inquirer is armed with amorous kindness. It argues a good deal to hide. . . .

At this precise moment—and it was strangely as if between us we had summoned him—I heard his unmistakable voice in the room beyond the studio, raised in an amiable shout of blended greeting and apology.

"In here," Lydia called. She took a step or two from the window and, without looking at me, took off the turban and shook out her hair. Mister Bowles came through into the studio, head inclined, as if to avoid an obstacle. "The door was open, you know," he said. "Oh, hello. I didn't know you had a visitor."

"Basil and I are old friends," Lydia said, contriving, with no doubt unconscious cruelty, to make this sound derogatory.

Mister Bowles looked at me for a moment or two, rather oddly I thought: not with that slight degree of humorous contempt her tone invited, but with a sort of indecision, as if this was something that would have to be taken into account.

He began moving slowly about the room. "My word," he said, "you have accumulated a lot of stuff." He was ill at ease, I could tell. I think the multiplicity of things bothered him, such a stark array of disparate objects in this unvarying light. He stopped from time to time to pick something up, turning to us with a sort of expostulation, humorous, but not altogether so. "What's this? And this? And what on earth is this?" Lydia replying point by point, a piece from an old olive press, a blue Iznik tile, as if justifying their presence there.

This went on for some time and was like a kind of game between them, like those games where something in the tone of voice identifies an object. I realize now that Mister Bowles was seeking, as usual, to impose himself on us and on the studio, establish his way of seeing things as the dominant one, the essential reality. His way of responding to the unfamiliar and daunting. On this occasion he was clearly failing. He could find no way of looking at this clutter of objects, no governing principle to account for their presence there—and he is a man who needs governing principles, I think, more than most. (Now, with the night silent beyond my shutters, in my area of inviolate lamplight, I remember again the stealthy hush of his room, the head, the revolver, the notebook. A governing principle there too, if I can find it.)

The performance was brought to an end by Lydia's asking if we would like a drink. There was German wine or Greek brandy. We both asked for wine. All the time Lydia was out of the room, Mister Bowles was moving restlessly about. He made some desultory remarks to me but my mind was not on his words. I noted the movements of his body; stiff, not ungraceful exactly, but inhibited, as if he felt a need for more room. His manner of touching things too was strange, unduly tentative. It was as though they might change texture or shape in his hands. It was not mere clumsiness, nor did it seem like that contained violence which often gives awkwardness to men's movements. It came to me then, Excellency, that Mister Bowles is not really at home in the world. It came to me with the force of a revelation. We are alike. I knew it from the beginning. Outwardly so dissimilar, yet we are deeply alike. So strong was this feeling that I experienced a violation, almost, of my own privacy and separateness. Doubtless we have come to it by different roads. In my case it is the trade of informing which has lost me the world. The role of informer severs in time all bonds. All action peters out except observing, interpreting. I am like a spent swimmer whose eyes and mind still register everything —everything, hue of sky, refractions and reflections of the water, line of the horizon—but who knows, throughout all this, that he is in the wrong element. (I can look downward, too, to the deep place where I shall presently drown.)

Mister Bowles has lost the world too, by courses which I can only guess at. He has lost, or perhaps he never had, essential familiarity with things, ease, custom. So of course he simulates, but badly, and this gives him a strange sort of dignity, power even; he imposes himself. Like a critical visitor. Or like a god, a minor god. A god would not, after all, move at ease among the inhabitants and artifacts of this world. He would be characterized by just this kind of hampered grace.

Lydia came back with the wine, in tall glasses. I sipped mine, still absorbed in my pure perception of Mister Bowles. He was standing with Lydia now. She was showing him the painting on the easel. They were close together, and had obviously ceased to be aware of me. I went through into the living room, where I had earlier noticed some grapes in a bowl on the sideboard. A handful of these I took to the window, and I stood there eating, looking out.

From here I could look inland, over the double row of acacia trees lining the avenue, to the white climbing houses of the town and the summits of Maron and Amphisea. Leros beyond, far off, but glowing clear in the morning light. The town, the whole island, was present to my mind, held in the protracted pang of its existence. For a few moments, standing there, my heart expanded with happiness. The cold wine, the sweet grapes, the indifferent beauty of the world, my recent *aperçu* about Mister Bowles, all combined to reconcile me. My clammy fears receded. I felt tenderness for those two standing together in the next room. More than tenderness. Love, Excellency. Love for them separately and together. And for all the people on the island, whatever the race or creed. As I finished the grapes there were tears in my eyes. I found a small piece of halvah on the sideboard and paused briefly at the door to eat it, before returning to the studio.

"You have captured," I heard Mister Bowles saying gravely, "the very essence of the landscape there."

They were still standing before Lydia's painting. I approached and looked closely at it again: white houses on the lower hillside, the Byzantine dome of Aghios Giorgos, cloaked shepherds, goats; the whole bathed in calmly radiant light.

"Yes, by Jove, you have caught it," Mister Bowles said, and it was true. Lydia had secured the landscape as effectively as if in some invisible noose. Or net. As always she had been faithful to the form and substance of things. As always she had failed to register what for me is the essence: the effects of a light so clear that it verges on the hallucinatory, cancelling those very perspectives that Lydia works so hard to achieve; the constant, half-surprised, half-acquiescent stirring of landscape and people into myth.

"I must confess," Mister Bowles said, "that I like paintings that grapple squarely with reality. Not try to dodge it, you know."

Lydia did not reply at once. She is not, after all, accustomed to talking about painting in terms of a wrestling match or a scrummage on the rugby field. Again I have the feeling that the Englishman's words belie him in some way. Is he simply a moralist, or does this praise of robust realism mask a sensibility he feels to be discreditable, unmanly?

"Well," Lydia said, "I believe myself that art should stay close to nature. That is the source of everything. These people in Paris now, Matisse and the *Fauves*, you know, they are causing quite a stir at the moment, but it is only a *succès de scandale*, it will fizzle out."

"I am not familiar with them," Mister Bowles said.

"Color for color's sake," Lydia said. You can't found a movement on that."

Mister Bowles nodded. His face expressed disapproval of these undisciplined Parisians. "Balance," he said. "Self-control. I have always understood these things to be fundamental. They are the classical virtues."

"Of course," Lydia said, "mere imitation is not . . . You must try to seize the essential nature of things, but the way is through attention to what is there, what is out there." She made a gesture toward the window.

Have you noticed, Excellency? *Capture. Catch. Grapple. Seize.* It is astonishing. Neither of them can talk about art for two minutes without using some such word. Odd, in extolling the classical virtues of balance and moderation, and opposing the exuberance of the colorists, odd that they should themselves use such frankly violent terms, words denoting assault and ravishment. I deal in reality myself, Excellency. Reality and illusion, their intimate blending. I have not attempted to disguise from your Excellency that my reports have not been entirely factual. But my effects are patiently and lovingly *contrived*—not imposed. To talk about truth as something that can be marched up to and arrested seems solemnly mad to me. Like one of your gendarmes trying to take Proteus into custody. You are left with something in your hands but not what you wanted. Lydia grasps her subjects too firmly, nothing has freedom, there is no potential for movement or change. The spectator also is immobilized. . . .

The violent apprehension of reality . . . We were still standing in front of the painting. Light flooded over us and over the room, evenly, impartially. Light filled my mind, drained, filled. The painting before me, a tract of land, an area of the mind, experience "seized" forever, no possibility of change; Mister Bowles, immobilized at last in this room of disturbing multiplicity, himself another *objet trouvé*; myself transfixed among unreadable signs and portents; and Lydia, Circe with the wand of her will, capturing our essences, stilling us forever in these arbitrary shapes. Homeric shadows touched my mind. As before, I felt the need to break out, assert autonomy of movement, speech. I said,

"You do not heighten reality by idealizing it, Lydia, if that is what you mean. And I suspect it is. It is idealization that does violence, not experiment, because it consumes its subject. It is dangerous in all departments. In love, in art, in politics. Conscious distortion is better."

"You mean telling lies," Mister Bowles said instantly. The man is a pure Manichaean. He sees everything in terms of moral opposites. Every conversation with him leads to head-on confrontations between darkness and light, good and evil.

"Telling lies?" I said. "No." Though half-smiling still, I felt myself becoming angry. "How have you arrived at this confident knowledge of what is lies and what is truth? I envy it."

"Kandinsky says color will express everything," Lydia said. "How do we know what colors are expressing?"

"Exactly," Mister Bowles said. "I mean to say, we know what a hay wain is, don't we?"

"I think free expression is dangerous," Lydia said. "I think it is a retrograde step. It simply encourages the irrational."

It was now that feeling betrayed me into indiscretion. I freely admit it, Excellency. The fact is that in all this talk of respect for reality, I began to smell again the swamp steam of your Empire, began to feel again that horror of immobility. "Not so dangerous," I said, "as trying to petrify things, even if you do it out of love. Not so violent as the means we use to contain the irrational, as you call it. Your paintings are violent, Lydia."

As soon as I had said this, I regretted it. I could see from Lydia's face that she was hurt—the severity of its repose once broken, her face has no guard against feeling. Besides this, I was weakening, faltering. My poor burst of fervor was over.

"That is absolute poppycock," Mister Bowles said. "Anyone with half an eye—"

Fortunately, at this point there was a brisk double knock on the living room door. Lydia left us and returned a moment later with Doctor Hogan. He had an arm over her shoulder. "Hallo, Basil my boy," he said, in his breezy way. "How's the old *stomachi?*"

"Fine," I said. "As an organ that is, not as an object of view." Some months ago I had persistent stomach pains, quite disabling. I thought at first they were due to dietary deficiencies consequent upon my poverty, but they turned out to be neurasthenic, the result of long hours of creative tension at my table here. The doctor provided me with a sedative syrup and I have been quite free of the pains since then.

"This is Mister Anthony Bowles," Lydia said. "Doctor Michael Hogan. Our beloved physician. Mister Bowles is a recent arrival on the island."

"I hope you enjoy your stay here." The doctor detached himself from Lydia to shake hands. I have described him before to your Excellency's officials. He stood now just inside the studio, bulky, untidy-looking, gray hair slightly disheveled as always, small blue eyes full of a cheerful guile.

"You are an old resident here, I take it," Mister Bowles said, his blurting habit of speech more noticeable now that he was addressing a stranger.

"Been here thirty years," the doctor said.

"He came here first on a cruise, didn't you, Michael?" Lydia said. "He liked it so much he decided to stay." She said this with evident pleasure and affection, making Mister Bowles a gift of it.

"That is about the sum of it," the doctor said.

Mister Bowles nodded, without much expression. It was not clear how he regarded this distant impulse of the doctor's.

"He had a practice in Dublin," Lydia said. "He went home, sold his practice, then came back here. Didn't you, Michael?"

"I've been here ever since," the doctor said.

It was at this point that I got up to go. Rather to my surprise, Mister Bowles offered to accompany me. Now, of course, I know why.

MISTER BOWLES'S reference to lying annoyed me at the time, because I suspected him of turning the conversation, with whatever it contained of interest or truth, into an occasion for establishing moral superiority. I still do suspect him of this, but I cannot yet decide whether it is the result of policy on his part, or personal need. Even after this morning's visit to the Pasha, I cannot decide.

I was feeling rather spruce, in my linen suit, with a clean white shirt buttoned up to the neck, my hair parted carefully with a wet comb, my monogrammed handkerchief and my ruby ring. Not having a watch now, I was afraid of being late. There is a clock in the shipping office of Gavros et Fils and that is the one I invariably go by, not because it keeps good time—in fact it doesn't—but because I prefer not to be confused by different versions. I glanced at this clock as I passed by, saw that I had time to spare and decided to walk the longer way, by the road. Plaints of sheep loud on the hillside. I saw the Petroulis boy herding sheep on the slope between the road and the shore. He will be bringing them into town today, to sell for the Sacrifice Bayram. He is about fourteen now, and good-looking.

I was on time at the Metropole and found Mister Bowles waiting in the lounge, sitting upright in a rattan chair. On the wall beyond him Zeus in the guise of a somewhat puny swan was descending on a Leda who looked quite capable of strangling him with one hand.

I could see that Mister Bowles too had taken extra care with his appearance this morning. He was wearing a gray suit of thin flannel, with rounded lapels in the English style. His collar was high and firm, and his dark green necktie carefully knotted. As he rose he took up a polished black cane from the floor beside his chair.

We walked across the square together to where the *fiacre*

drivers wait, in the shade of the municipal acacia trees. Costas Gavroulis was at the head of the line. I was afraid he would refuse me as a passenger, but he agreed at once to take us, though his manner was surly. We climbed into the creaking carriage, settled our backs against the seamed brown leather; the driver whipped up his stringy chestnut mare, and we moved sedately off. The smell of the dying acacia blossom was heavy in the air; morning sunshine fell through the thin leaves onto the buckles of the harness, onto the marigolds twisted in the bridle, and onto Mister Bowles and me sitting side by side.

We kept to the lower road, which follows the line of the bay, for some time, in the direction away from the promontory, away from the ruins that Mister Bowles is interested in, before turning inland. On our right the long fluid line of Mt. Leros, and on the other side the blue water of the bay.

We did not talk much on the way. The Pasha's house is on the northern side of the island, where the hills come in nearer to the shore, dip toward the sea in long slopes that have been terraced for vines and olives. In the narrow fertile strip between hills and shore, maize and vegetables grow well, and there are extensive orange groves. All this land, whether tended by Greek or Turk, belongs to the Pasha. After a mile or so, the road begins to climb and curve inland, into the foothills. The Pasha's house and the garrison barracks are on the landward side, soon after this curve begins. The house is set well back from the road, its white walls only partially visible beyond clumps of umbrella pines.

The driver set us down on the road—he was unwilling to turn into the drive. We asked him to wait, and passed through the wrought iron gates, open and unguarded. The driveway is short. It opens directly on the house, which is wide-fronted, Italianate in style, with steps going up to a colonnaded entrance. To the right, separated by sparse shrubbery, the dusty desolate expanse of the parade ground with the barracks and outbuildings beyond.

At the foot of the steps a soldier with a slung rifle emerged from a sentry-box and barred our way. He said nothing, asked us no questions, simply stood silently in front of us effectively barring all further progress. Young, not more than twenty I should think, with a flat, expressionless Anatolian face. After a moment or two of impassive scrutiny, he unslung the rifle and held it loosely before him, pointing somewhere between Mister Bowles and me.

"We have an appointment to see the Commandant," I said to him in Turkish, taking care to stand quite still—I had not at all liked his gesture with the rifle. The garrison troops are ill-trained, Excellency, and they are unhappy, for the most part, on this western island, far from the plateaus of home. They do not like the people here, least of all foreigners. And the recent ambushes, the deaths of their comrades, have unsettled them even further. It seemed to me within the bounds of possibility for this savage to shoot us. Mister Bowles, however, obviously not thinking along the same lines as myself, took an impatient step forward. The rifle swung upward. It was now pointing at Mister Bowles's chest.

"This is ridiculous," Mister Bowles said. His face had flushed darkly beneath the tan. He showed no sign of fear. "Tell the fool to let us pass," he said.

Fortunately at this moment Izzet Effendi appeared at the top of the steps. He spoke sharply to the guard, who even then hesitated noticeably before turning back.

At the top of the steps I introduced Mister Bowles. "They are overzealous," Izzet said, in his dry querulous voice, in part apology for the behavior of the guard. He looked carefully at Mister Bowles. "Tell him," he said, "these days we must be on our guard. There are many undesirable persons on the island, professional revolutionaries, agents of all kinds. They are receiving support from foreign powers, among whom, regrettably, we must include the English. Indeed the English are prominent among them. They are anarchists, dangerous people."

"Tell him," Mister Bowles said, when this had been explained to him, "that there are not many anarchists in the House of Commons as yet."

It was the first thing approaching a joke that I had heard him say. I did not translate it, however. I said simply that Mister Bowles quite understood the situation.

Izzet led us inside, through a small anteroom, into the reception room, where we sat in uncomfortable brocaded chairs. Izzet inquired about the state of things in England. Mister Bowles spoke about Mr. Asquith's government. While this went on I was able to look around the room, survey the fruits of office: gilt rococo tables, jade boxes, a large ormolu and gold clock with a decorative frame of cherubs around a central sun, a grand piano, silk roses under a glass dome. Excellency, I wonder if you know what injustice and malpractice of every sort is represented by these expensive European imports? Every inch of alabaster and rosewood is charged with suffering. Their sounds, if they could make sounds, would be a shriek. In fact, in the pauses of conversation, I seemed to hear it, this shriek of extortion. My ears have become sensitive, now that my days are running out.

Harmony depends on a balance of forces. I must accept this, must put away my sick doubts, my longing to sabotage the scales. Pythagoras stressed it, everyone has subsequently admitted it. But while harmony may characterize the universe as a whole, as a self-regulating principle, in human affairs we must do our own regulating. A certain abuse of power is only to be expected. But not Steinways, Excellency. For Mahmoud Pasha to burden the peasants in order to acquire a grand piano his thick fingers cannot play and his malformed ears cannot appreciate, that is when harmony breaks down, in every sense of the word; that is a discord impossible not to dwell on.

These thoughts were passing through my mind, when the Pasha came in and we stood up for introductions. The Pasha took three steps toward Mister Bowles before stopping. Quite a high mark of respect. Mister Bowles had to take five or six steps to shake his hand. I have seen him often enough before, but always on public occasions, in uniform, breast resplendent with medals. Here in his house he looked grosser, the shape of his head blunter, more elemental. Perhaps with a dim sense that this was a cultural occasion, he was wearing, instead of uniform, a black Stambouli frock coat, strained tight across his thick shoulders. His small, incurious eyes surveyed us both steadily for some moments, then he said, "Hos bolduk," in a voice rasping and slow and I replied, as etiquette demanded, "Hos geldenez."

We seated ourselves again, and remained for some time in a silence broken only by the faint wheeze of the Pasha's breathing and the shrieks of his acquisitions. The blinds were drawn against the morning sunlight, but the slats were open, so that the room was patterned with light. Mister Bowles's lowered head, his eyebrows and moustache, were gilded, my hands in my patient lap were striped with light. From my right, where the courtyard would be, I heard the graded tinkling of water, falling from different levels in the fountain. From elsewhere, in the interior of the house, came the voices of women, raised in what sounded like a plaintive altercation.

Izzet began to speak. It was a question, he said, was it not, if he and the Pasha understood matters aright, it was a question of a lease of some kind . . . some part of the coastal area included in the Pasha's possessions. . . . The vagueness, of course, was deliberate. All bargaining in the Levant begins and ends on a note of aristocratic indifference.

I explained the Englishman's proposition once again. I knew, of course, that desire for profit was at the moment contending in their breasts with distrust of the foreigner. There might be other reasons for wanting to obtain free access to coastal territory—reasons which an occupying power would be quick to suspect. And there was after all something strange—in view of the time and place—almost excessive, in the very legality of Mister Bowles's proceeding.

Because of all this, and just as had happened in my interview with Izzet earlier, I found myself seeking to allay their suspicions by stressing the Englishman's simplicity and sincerity, his deep faith in the processes of law. This meant, in effect, making him out as something of a simpleton—the equivalent in commercial terms of a holy fool.

They listened, the Pasha in total, basilisk immobility, Izzet directing his thin face from time to time toward the Englishman. Both deeply dishonest men, they were naturally finding it hard to understand Mister Bowles. Nothing changed in the Pasha while I spoke—he might have been sleeping—but I thought I detected a growing, predatory intentness in Izzet: the Englishman's simple faith in legality was working its magic with him.

"Tell them," Mister Bowles said, leaning forward earnestly, "that I should feel myself to be trespassing on the Pasha's property if I had not paid a proper sum for the right of access."

"He wants everything done in the proper way," I said. "You know the English sense of fair play. *Dürüst hareket.* It is known the world over."

"*Biliorium,*" the Pasha said. "*Türkler gibbi.* In this they resemble us Turks." He inclined his thick body forward. The movement brought into prominence the bulk of his revolver holster under the frock coat. "You will take coffee?" he said.

Izzet went out to order it and there was silence until he returned. Then I said, "He is willing to pay, of course. A nominal fee."

"Nominal?" Izzet leaned forward with a snap at the word.

"He is not seeking to buy the land, only to acquire a short lease on it. A lease of one month."

Mister Bowles must have sensed that we had reached the stage of discussing money for he said suddenly, in his light, blurting voice, "I was thinking in the region of two hundred liras."

I sought to cover up my consternation. This was far more than the land was worth. Fortunately at this point the coffee was brought in, by a soldier in uniform but bareheaded, and some time passed in the usual politeness.

"Listen," I said to Mister Bowles, when we were again settled, "you are offering too much. Leave things to me."

To my amazement, Mister Bowles frowned and shook his head. "Offer them two hundred liras," he said. "That seems to me a fair price."

"But it is more than the land could be sold for," I said. After all, he had charged me with the affair, and I was unwilling to sit by and allow him to be despoiled. "Such an offer will make them suspicious," I said.

"I think not," Mister Bowles said. "Please do as I ask."

"Very well," I said. I felt some degree of contempt for this obstinacy. "He offers two hundred liras for the lease," I said to Izzet, and saw his eyes flicker.

Neither he nor Mahmoud Pasha said anything for some time, but I saw almost at once that Mister Bowles had been right: they were not suspicious, they were merely, out of long habit, pretending to consider. Two hundred liras for a short lease on a few hectares of steep and stony ground, no doubt acquired only incidentally in the first place! No, they were not suspicious. I had done my preliminary work almost too well. The Englishman, they had decided, was in earnest, was a fool, was rich. The combination had gone to their heads. Their attempts at judiciousness, at the appearance of a bargaining stance, would not have deceived a child.

It deceived Mister Bowles, however, apparently, because he said suddenly, "I could perhaps improve on that."

"No, no," I said hastily. "No, they will accept."

I saw them glance at each other. Then Izzet turned to me and said, "*Tamam*. The *Vali* accepts the offer."

The Pasha leaned forward again. "As a gesture," he said in his rasping voice, "of friendship—" This speech was never finished, because at this moment a servant entered, a civilian in red headcloth and *entari*, and spoke some words very softly, leaning close to the Pasha. Listening hard, I thought I heard the name of Gesing, the commercial agent. At once Mahmoud Pasha addressed himself to the business of rising. Finally on his feet before us, he uttered excuses, something required his attention, he would return.

He did not return, however, and the rest of our business was conducted with Izzet alone. Not that much was left to do. I told Izzet that Mister Bowles would require a form of contract.

"Is that really necessary?" he said. "The Pasha has given his word."

I did not dare to laugh, though I was inclined to. "He asks if the contract is necessary," I said to Mister Bowles.

He nodded vigorously. "Absolutely," he said. He stood up and smiled at us both. I do not think I had seen him smile before. Not counting polite stretchings of the lips. It was a gradual smile, deepening slowly, as if backed up by afterthoughts; and as he smiled his eyes widened slightly, in a way that was unusual and very engaging. "Making out a contract is the proper thing to do," he said. "It serves as mutual protection."

"He says he must have one," I said.

"*Olur*," Izzet said, with resignation. It was clear that he did not at all like the idea of the contract, though I find it difficult to see why.

"When will it be ready?" I said.

"In some days. When can he pay the money?"

"I can pay a deposit," Mister Bowles said. "Say five per-cent of the total. When the contract is signed, that is. The balance may take a few days longer. I shall have to effect a transfer from my bank in London through the Ottoman Bank in Constantinople and then to the bank's agent on the island." He hesitated for a moment, then said, "I did not expect to need so much money here."

Was it the pause, the addition, that made me doubt him? He was not given to explaining himself. Surely, if he were writing a book, as he says, he must have anticipated some such expenditure. Perhaps, of course, he did not realize that the ruins were so extensive.

Izzet did not look very happy, either, when I translated. Still, five percent is not bad, considering the exorbitant price of the lease. If Izzet was thinking of delaying the contract till the balance arrived, Mister Bowles's next words put an end to such hopes. "The contract must be ready for tomorrow," he said, "so that I can get started. I have no intention of arranging for the transfer until the contract is signed."

"Very well." Izzet shrugged his thin shoulders. "You will call for the contract at my office," he said to me. "Shall we say at five?"

Izzet accompanied us to the foot of the steps, past the silent soldier in his box. There we shook hands and left him.

In the *fiacre*, on the way home, Mister Bowles and I sat as before, side by side, but I felt a difference. What had happened in the room behind us had made us, in a way I found difficult to define, accomplices.

I think it was Gesing's name I heard, Excellency. I am almost sure of it. He must be important in some way: Mahmoud Pasha rose almost with alacrity at those few whispered words.

The curiosity about the message remains with me. As does that faint suspicion of Mister Bowles—not suspicion exactly, but a feeling of complicity, of being leagued with him in some enterprise the nature of which I have not yet fully understood. That day in Lydia's studio I felt something of this. A kind of acknowledgment. From the very first day, the day of his arrival, I felt included in his purposes.

The Greeks do not speak to me, Excellency. They do not look at me. In their minds they have written *finis* to me. I trail silence with me wherever I go. I am insubstantial to myself. Only here, in this room, where the silence is of my own contriving, only here do I assume my gravity of flesh. Only when writing am I real to myself, and only then is my death completely real to me. It is here I experience my worst fear of death. I look at my hands, so cunning, feel my weight on the chair. My mind orders the words . . . I will insist on coherence up to the moment of my death. My only courage not to gibber.

Sometimes I dream of getting off the island, getting to Constantinople, finding out what has happened to my reports. I would dedicate it to you, Excellency. My book.

There is material for several volumes. I have not yet decided on a title. When I think of this possibility, this crowning of all my life's work, my heart expands with delight. Everything, then, would have been worth it, poverty, loneliness, my narrow life. But it will not happen.

Meanwhile the days succeed one another, days of summer. Hazy mornings, glittering noons, velvet evenings. I wake with the light and seat myself here early, while the mist still lies along the join between the nearer islands and the sea, and along the distant promontories of Asia. I sit here watching this beautiful interaction, this *complicity*—that word again—between sea and sky, the way the hazes soften the complicated folds and recesses of land—as if these willful masses needed protecting, the sharp promontories needed sheathing.

The sea is always present to me, whether within sight or not; there on the limits of my existence, glimmering in delicate perspectives or standing brilliant and vertical on the same plane as the sky; there as an element in the light, imparting its own quality of radiance. This pervasiveness of the sea, common to all small islands, gives a provisional quality to life. Exquisite matings of earth, water and air gave us our being here, and still they lived in a *ménage à trois*, without those disillusionments said to be inevitable. If there is ever a real quarrel we shall be engulfed. Meanwhile the dalliance continues, a game of creation in which islands on the horizon and islands in the sky are glimpsed, surmised, lost again, and shapes of land lodge, swim, dissolve. Out there, far away, on the farthest verge of vision and beyond, other beings inhabit those fleeting shapes, and from their stillness—which seems like motion to me—they are watching with wonder the short-lived shape on which I count for permanency.

It is no wonder Excellency, that so many philosophers have come from this world—Ionia or the nearer islands. I mean the artist-philosophers who tried to interpret the universe. Not riddling, posturing Socrates, stroking his beard and asking for definitions. Detestable man. No, I mean those who came before that. Faced with the manifold illusion of the senses, the paradox of permanence and change, in this light at once clear and deceiving, they sought always for an *extreme* explanation, a principle of unity. What a leap of the mind that was, Excellency. What a giant stride. They freed us from matter, to which, of course, with modern science, we are again subjected. Those who talk of the Greek sense of balance, of the Golden Mean, forget these holy extremists. It is in extremes that the true Greek spirit lies. Pythagoras, Empedocles, Heraclitus, Anaximander—the very names have a delightful cadence. I see them standing on these shores seeking to reconcile all apparent contradictions in a single dazzling formula. Parmenides is perhaps the one who best suits our condition, yours and mine, Excellency, as he suits all who fear dissolution. He says that motion itself is an illusion. The lunge of the knife, the revolts of subject states, illusory.

I have seen Mister Bowles again. Not half an hour ago I saw him, walking along the shore below my house. He was going toward the headland, as usual. Presumably he will follow the same procedure as before, climb up into the hills from the far end of the bay. It must take him three hours at least of strenuous walking, over difficult terrain, to reach the ruins up there. There are no paths. No one goes there much now. Certainly it cannot be denied that Mister Bowles is an enthusiast for research.

He has the contract now, at least. I took him two copies, having first checked the wording with Izzet. It was written in Arabic characters, and extremely convoluted in style. However, the area in question was precisely delineated; it was specified that no building operations of any kind were to be undertaken, nor any work of mining or excavation to be carried out; the sums were correctly stated, and the dates of the lease; each copy bore the signature of the Pasha, and the official seal.

"I like everything to be clear and aboveboard, you know," Mister Bowles said, when I gave him the papers.

"I, on the other hand," I said politely, "prefer a certain degree of fruitful murk."

"How do you make that out?" he said negligently. He had not expressed any thanks for the trouble I was taking on his behalf, nor had he referred again to the question of a fee for my services. Ridiculously enough, I could not remind him, Excellency; I still want his respect, still nurse some remnants of that feeling I had at first, that he might like me, that we might become friends. We were in the lounge, under the sternly lecherous eye of Prussian Zeus.

"I do not think human beings can live for very long above the board," I said. "The light would shrivel them up."

Mister Bowles laughed at this, an explosive sound. He was smoking a thin cheroot, but did not offer me one. "Everything strives for light," he said. "Everything."

"Possibly," I said. "But striving for light is the natural result of normally preferring darkness."

He laughed again. He seemed to be in a jovial mood. Perhaps his researches are going well. "I can sign this with a clear mind anyway," he said. "Since you tell me it is all in order."

I was pleased that he trusted me. So pleased that my grievance about the fee receded. Mister Bowles has some quality of binding people to him.

"They didn't ask for it to be signed in their presence then," he said. "No, of course not—the contract does not matter much to them, does it."

This remark showed a shrewdness that surprised me. Mister Bowles is full of surprises. . . . I took Izzet his copy back at once, together with the ten liras which had been agreed on as a deposit.

"Mister Bowles would like a receipt for this," I said.

"He is a great one for papers," Izzet said sourly. "Does he say when the balance of the money will be arriving?"

"No."

Izzet looked at me for a moment in silence. Now that we were alone together he was much less friendly. "The Pasha will hold you personally responsible," he said.

"I merely acted as interpreter," I told him.

"You will be held responsible," he said again.

We parted coldly. I was depressed and frightened by his words, Excellency. I know what can happen to those against whom Mahmoud Pasha has a grievance. I could not settle down to my report in the evening—I lost a valuable evening's writing time because of that cursed Izzet. Gone forever the words I might have written then. The mood of one day is never like that of the next.

Today I feel better. I now have my month's pay in hand, collected this morning from Pariente, the local agent for the Banque Ottomane. This is paid on the fifth day of the month with absolute regularity. It has not varied, to my recollection, for twenty years and is, in itself, I sometimes think, an argument for a regulated universe, with all controls set. Pariente is a melancholy man at the best of times, and I thought he looked at me with some special quality of sorrow today. Again I wondered if he was the leak, if it was he I had to thank for my predicament.

"Keeping you busy this week," I said to him, in jocular reference to the well-known fact that his post is not very exacting. "First the Englishman, and now me."

"Englishman?" he said. Pariente's eyes are chestnut brown, luxuriantly lashed. There was no flicker of comprehension in them as he looked back at me, and I knew in that moment, quite beyond any doubt, that Mister Bowles had not so far been to see him to arrange a transfer. Interesting fact, Excellency.

From there I went to the Sans Souci for an apéritif. At this stage in the month I always allow myself such gestures —it is good for the morale. I tried to engage Stavros, the waiter, in conversation, but he barely spoke to me. In fact, he walked away from me while I was still speaking. After an acquaintance of nine years, Excellency.

I have been thinking again about the American, and

about Lydia's words and behavior that afternoon at her studio, that unguarded remark of hers, that she *had heard of him*. Surely that can only mean she knew of him beforehand, before he came here. Unless it was simply a fault in her English, the wrong choice of preposition. But no, she was conscious herself of having said the wrong thing, she tried to cover it up by talking of the Italian crew-member. Where can she have learned of Mister Smith's existence? Presumably on her travels.

She was disappointed—and annoyed—to hear they had searched the boat. That was because they had botched the business. So she had wanted Mister Smith to be detected. But in what? Excellency, it can only be guns, or arms of some kind. What else would he be waiting there for? Spargos, Ramni, all the islands to the west, belong now to the Greeks. What could be easier than for a boat to put out from there? A meeting out in the bay some moonless night, the cargo transferred to Mister Smith's caïque. He is here as a bona fide sponge fisherman. All he has to do is wait for the right opportunity. A rendezvous with the rebels from the interior, a *barca* rowed across the bay. Beyond the headland there are numerous inlets suitable for the purpose . . .

But if this is indeed the truth of the matter, and Lydia has definite knowledge of it, then it is highly probable that she warned the authorities herself. Perhaps this is how she lives so free from interference on the island. She travels, she hears things, she passes them on. Not for pay, like a professional, but for love. . . . I remember the passion of her opposition to change, new styles in art. Perhaps she feels the same about political changes. Lydia is on your side, Excellency, it would seem. A natural reactionary. Or is it that she dislikes people making money out of guns? Instruments of death, as she would probably put it.

Now, forewarned in his turn, Mister Smith might change his plans, even decide to abandon the attempt. Or, depending on his psychology, he will feel emboldened. Quite possible, of course, that I am wrong about him, wrong about Lydia. What is it based on, after all? An uncertain inflec-

85

tion, a momentary loss of poise, an odd choice of phrase. Slight indications indeed. All the same, there *was* something . . . She was waiting for him, for Mister Bowles. She was excited. Is she in love with him? Perhaps it was excitement that disturbed her judgment, betrayed her into those small, but revealing, indiscretions.

I will keep my eyes on them, Excellency.

Just after midnight. I hear the first whistles of the night watchmen. An instructive evening, Excellency. I was making for the Metropole with no particular intention in mind, and I had just reached the small *plateia* below it, when I saw a group of people, among them Lydia and Herr Gesing, sitting on the terrace of the *taverna* on the far side—*Ta Varelia*, it is called, Excellency. It has a terrace with a grapevine, and colored lanterns, a pretty place. I hesitated for some moments, but I did not think there would be any trouble from the Greeks while I was in that company—the worst they could do was refuse to serve me. I walked across the *plateia*, observing as I drew nearer that Dr. Hogan and his wife were in the group—he is married to a woman of the island. Also the French engineer Chaudan, and another lady, whom I did not know. There was no one else on the terrace—they had put two tables together, so they could all sit round.

Doctor Hogan was the first to see me. "Hallo, Basil," he said. "Come and join us."

"This is Mrs. Marchant," Lydia said. "She is traveling in this part of the world. Basil Pascali, one of the fixtures of the island."

"Slightly more mobile than that, I hope," I said, bowing to Mrs. Marchant, who is a woman of about fifty, with narrow gray eyes and a very full underlip. I sat down next to her with Lydia on the other side of me. I was curious about Mrs. Marchant. There is no cruise ship in at present, Excellency. She must be traveling alone and independently. Not so unusual for a woman these days as it used to be, but all the same . . .

"You are lucky to be living here," she said. Her accent was American. From the folds of her person, released by this little stirring of enthusiasm, came odors of warm, scented crepe.

"Oh, Basil is a gentleman of leisure," Doctor Hogan said. He is a genial fellow, but like the others, thinks of me as an idle sponger. Amusing. A fixture of the island. An unfortunate phrase, in view of my predicament. Lydia, however, knows me better than the others. She knows my feelings for her, though these have never been expressed in words. She senses my sufferings.

"It is such a *spiritual* landscape, so infused with *spirit*," Mrs. Marchant said. "Anyone who lives here, as you do, must be touched with spirit, you cannot be immune."

"Spirit," Herr Gesing said, before I could reply. "Yes, *meine Dame,* but what is this spirit, I ask you, this word that people talk about so . . ."

"Freely?" I suggested, back to my old game of completing Herr Gesing's thoughts for him.

"Freely, *ja.*"

His voice was thickened with the wine he had been drinking. Before Mrs. Marchant could reply, Lydia looked up and said, "Ah here you are, Anthony." The tall figure of the Englishman was standing silently before us. First-name terms, Excellency. We had not seen him approach. He must have come from above, by way of the steps. In those first few moments I looked at Lydia's face, rather than at him, and saw on it a look of vivid expectation. There was something vulnerable, exposed, about her expression. I was reminded of her devotional look in the studio. In spite of her worldliness, she trusts people with her feelings, trusts to their good will, as children do. Very dangerous.

"Sorry I'm late," Mister Bowles said. They had arranged to meet, then. He sat down on the other side of Lydia.

"By spirit I was referring to the higher feelings," Mrs. Marchant said. "All that is not material. Our moral sense. Our sense of beauty for example . . ."

Herr Gesing said brusquely, "Spirit is *Geist,* no? It is not feeling, it is movement. Through all history it is working. Like a turbine. Not the machine, you understand, the energy principle. Hegel, it was Hegel, who—"

"Energy principle?" Lydia broke in. "What does that mean? You're as bad as Basil, the other day, defending free expression. That's another kind of energy principle, I suppose. None of you will look at what is before your eyes. I believe in *things*. You talk as if the world were empty. All these energy principles and swirling movements in history. It is simply opening the floodgates."

"Floodgates to what?" Doctor Hogan said.

"To the irrational."

"Floodgates?" Herr Gesing said.

I could not recall the German for this, so attempted to convey the idea by gesture and explanation.

"Ah, *die Schleusen*," Herr Gesing said. "Do you know Stefan George?

"Auf die Schleusen
Und aus Rusen
Regnen Rosen
Güsse Flüsse
Die begraben."

"Good God," Mister Bowles said, presumably in some sort of reproof or embarrassment at this public display.

"The irrational isn't outside somewhere, waiting to flood in," Doctor Hogan said. "You are doing the same thing as our friend here, creating abstractions."

"That is true," Monsieur Chaudan said, inclining his head politely. "It is not separated. The rational and the irrational, *ils habitent le même corps*."

"The same body," Doctor Hogan said. "That is somehow a frightening idea. Like running from a demon to your own safe room and locking the door, and finding the demon locked in with you."

Mister Bowles cleared his throat. "Was it a profitable practice?" he said suddenly. "The one you gave up, I mean." The question came oddly, at this juncture. At first I interpreted its severely practical tone as a protest against the general nature of the conversation, which he was perhaps finding uncomfortably literary; but I realized almost at once that in fact it marked the degree to which Mister Bowles had been impressed by the sacrifice of material interest the doctor had made by settling here all those years ago.

It took Doctor Hogan, engaged as he was in the conversation with Chaudan, several moments to understand what Mister Bowles was driving at. Then he said, "Yes, reasonably so. Why do you ask?"

"Well, I am a practical man," Mister Bowles said. "These things have to be taken into account when we are making decisions. We can't just throw everything overboard."

"That depends on the nature of the cargo and the state of the weather." The doctor looked away from Mister Bowles toward his wife, who was sitting opposite. They smiled at each other.

"Yes, but just a minute," Mister Bowles said. He was obviously intending to press the matter further, but at this point, quite audibly, though distant, we heard the sound of male voices chanting. It came from somewhere above us, in the main part of the town.

"Now what is that?" Mrs. Marchant said.

"Tomorrow is Saint Alexi's Day," I explained to her. "He is the patron saint of the island. A local saint, you know. They don't bother about him anywhere else. They have the custom here of bearing him in effigy around the town, on the evening before. Then he is left in the church all night."

"That sounds mighty interesting," Mrs. Marchant said.

With a very unattractive disregard for the present trend of the conversation, and in particular for Mrs. Marchant, who was waiting to hear more of Saint Alexi, Herr Gesing now abruptly returned to his former topic. "No, no," he said loudly, "*Geist* is to *Gischt* related, the white of the sea. Always moving. Perhaps also it is to *Gäscht* related, that is in the bread, to make it rise up. Again, you see, the movement, the fermending. *Verstehen Sie?*"

"Fermenting," I said.

"The French word does not signify anything of that kind," Monsieur Chaudan said, looking at Herr Gesing coldly.

The German raised his face of a plump hawk. "Not surprise," he said. "Your language is poor in many ways. *Wiedergeburt*, for example, you have no word for *Wiedergeburt*."

"Rebirth," I said.

"Rebirth, *ja*. In French there is not this idea. *Renaissance*, it is not the same. That is a word without blood or flesh in it."

"What I mean is," Mister Bowles said to the doctor, totally ignoring Herr Gesing, "we must keep a firm hold on reality. You know, both feet on the ground. I suppose a lot depends on nationality, really."

There was a certain crassness in this that made me look quickly at Lydia, but her face reflected no consciousness of it. The doctor smiled at Mister Bowles, but not with great warmth. "You do not have the look of a realist," he said, "if you will forgive me saying so. And I don't think, myself, that the English are such a realistic people as all that. Not like the French, for example."

"I can't agree with you," Mister Bowles said stiffly.

"We have no words for stupid abstractions, *ça c'est vrai*," Monsieur Chaudan said to Herr Gesing in a tone of anger. "Stupid and dangerous also. *On n'en a pas besoin*. We don't need them."

I heard the chanting again, this time much nearer. Herr Gesing looked down at his plate. He did not reply to the Frenchman. When he looked up again it was on Mister Bowles that he fixed his eyes.

"The researches," he said. "They are going well?"

Mister Bowles looked briefly at me. Then he transferred his gaze back to the German. "Yes," he said. "Very well." His hands as they lay on the table, and one side of his face, were tinted pale crimson from the lantern over his head. Small moths fluttered against the panes of the lanterns, clung there, or fell back dazed among the vine leaves.

"How did you know about it?" Mister Bowles said.

Herr Gesing made a small gesture with one hand. "Somebody was speaking about it," he said. "You go there often," he said. "Every day. It is interesting for you, yes?" he said.

"Very interesting," Mister Bowles said. Deliberately he looked away from Herr Gesing, back to Doctor Hogan. "We have always been known as a practical people," he said.

"Practical is not the same as realistic," the doctor said. "You have ideas of things, always formed beforehand somehow. So you don't look closely. As if you had dreamed it. Then you try to shape things in accordance with the dream. It's all right when it fits, but if the matter proves recalcitrant, you become unreasonable. Very unreasonable." The doctor paused, looking across at Mister Bowles with his habitual expression, cheerful, sly rather—but without real malice. "The Irish know that to their cost," he said. "Cromwell was a great dreamer."

Mister Bowles was visibly not pleased by these words, but before he could say anything in reply our attention was distracted by the appearance on the square, to our right, of Saint Alexi on his litter, borne by six men and preceded by two priests with censers. They walked in silence now. Oil lamps at either side of the saint's face lit up the yellow composure of his features. His arms in cloth of gold were crossed over his breast. Light from the lamps fell on the faces of the bearers, and they too had a set, waxen appearance, like the saint's mourning offspring. They walked the length of the square and disappeared from view.

"What is he made of?" Mrs. Marchant said.

"Wax," I replied. "A good seventy years old at that."

"I really am fascinated by these age-old religious practices," Mrs. Marchant said. "They seem to embody the whole spirit of a people."

"Tomorrow evening in the church, they enact his Assumption," I said. "Rather an interesting ceremony in its way. If you would like to see it I'll accompany you, with pleasure."

I suppose it was rash of me to commit myself to a public appearance, but I have a faint hope of something from Mrs. Marchant. Love, money. Preferably both. A very faint hope—I am not everybody's *beau idéal*. Penniless, possessed, pursued Pascali. I need a benefactress if anyone does. Besides, I am beginning to sicken of my fears. I will show my face boldly in the church.

Mrs. Marchant at once closed with my offer; the arrangement was made. Shortly afterward Lydia and she and Mister Bowles went off together. The Hogans left. Chaudan, too. I rose with alacrity. I did not want to be left alone with Herr Gesing. He had seen the look Mister Bowles gave me. He would question me.

"Ah," he said, as I stood there. "The great interpreter."

"Yes," I said. "As you say."

Herr Gesing nodded his head slowly. He was a little drunk. "The linguist," he said.

"Yes," I said. "Polyglot, perverted, of mixed descent, you behold in me the perfect Ottoman gentleman."

Nervousness made me flippant, Excellency. He looked at me in silence for a while, then he said, "This lease, this famous lease, it is not legal, Pascali. It is not *valid*. It was not for them . . . He has no right."

"In that case . . ." I said.

He raised one broad, short-fingered hand. "No," he said. "There are other interests . . ."

"Involved?"

"Involved, *ja*. He must be persuaded, Pascali. Quietly. From the land . . . removed. It is dangerous for him."

Herr Gesing moved his hand loosely back and forth several times. "You do this for me," he said. "I will pay you."

"I'll see what I can do," I said.

He nodded, but said nothing more. I wished him good night, and walked away.

Here now in the silence of my room, dawn threatening beyond the shutters, it is not the German's talk of danger, nor his offer of money, that occupies my mind. I do not see how I can earn the money. Besides, if he had real power, he would not appeal to me, despised Pascali. No, what I chiefly recall are the enmities running below the surface of that conversation, barely kept in check by manners. Traits of character, resources of language, used alike for assertions of national superiority. A little glimpse of the cockpit, Excellency. Then the American lady, taking a moral view. Even our resident Celt, the good doctor, normally so equable, allowed himself to blame Mister Bowles for the misfortunes of Ireland.

All the same there is something in what he said about the English, their capacity for dreaming. Look at their great colony of India, so many diverse races, so many millions, held in thrall. That is a continent in the grip of an alien dream, dream of destiny, dream of glory. How else to explain it? Not like your possessions, Excellency—those are lands of simple conquest, administered by the greatest bureaucracy the world has ever known. Admittedly this bureaucracy has now become petrified at an advanced stage of corruption. But after five hundred years what will theirs be like? It will not last so long. No one can dream so long.

Noon, Excellency. I must write fast if I am to finish my account of this morning before the time arranged for the meeting with Mrs. Marchant. Forgive me if the style is slipshod.

Not a creditable morning for me, Excellency. Indeed, in a way, disgraceful. I am reluctant, really, to dwell on it. However, dwell on it I must. Every informer worth his salt must linger over distasteful matter sometimes. Even excrement can provide clues, if expertly prodded and sniffed. It is an obscure form of heroism for which we seldom get credit.

The fact is that I followed Mister Bowles and Lydia along the shore. It was not actually so planned and deliberate as this might sound—I must be careful not to give the wrong impression. They set off on horseback early, soon after the sun had risen, she riding easily on a chestnut mare, Mister Bowles stiff and awkward on a slightly restive gray-and-white gelding. (These horses belong to Cavit Oksuz, whose brother was sent to prison only a month ago for shooting a man on the mainland, at Cismeh—some quarrel over a woman.) She was dressed for riding, in jodhpurs and boots. Mister Bowles, however, wore only a gray pullover and gray flannel trousers. He had on a cloth cap also, like those King Edward wears.

They passed along the shore below my window. I was only just awake, after some two or three hours of troubled sleep—I cannot sleep for long these days. No doubt they were intending to ride beside the sea until they reached the rocky parts below the headland, then turn their horses inland, up into the hills, thus following Mister Bowles's normal route. At least this is what I pretended to think, in order to give myself grounds for suspicion.

They rode at the verge of the water, now on the wet shingle, now allowing the horses' hooves to dip and flash in the shallows of the waves—hardly waves, brief grainy flaws in the surface. The sea brimmed with light, light held steady by the slight haze, not shed or spilled in any glints of brilliance. The sun was clear of the sea, but still trammeled in the dawn mist, not yet streaming off into the sky. Through this soft, luminous light they went, keeping the horses at a walking pace. They looked like conquerors, Excellency. Beyond them, awaiting their pleasure, the peaks and dromedary shapes of the mountains.

I watched them pass along the bay, watched first with my unaided eyes, then with Signor Niccoli's telescope. And when they were no longer visible, when they had dissolved in the fluid distance, I brooded on their passing. My room, scene of my labors over the years, scene of triumphs of a higher order than that of mere physical *superbia*, yet seemed cramped and mean to me, the hole at the end of my burrowing life. I looked at my miserable paraphernalia of pleasure, books, hookah, coffee cup and bowl; at my shabby clothes and unkempt person, still sour from sleep. A kind of rebellious misery rose in me. Why should I sit here, hatching other people's motives and purposes?

In short, Excellency, I decided to follow them, to see what

took them out riding so early. Even then, while I was still preparing to go out, even then I knew that I was deceiving myself, knew that I was committing a cardinal sin of informers, acting not out of professional curiosity, at least not mainly, but out of jealousy and pain. I knew what took them out so early. However, the decision once made, I lost no time. My linen suit I thought unsuitable, forgive the pun, too conspicuous against the hillsides. I put on my old jacket and trousers, lamentably crumpled and baggy, and on my head a dark gray headcloth, tied in the Turkish fashion. My shoes with the heels bent down into slippers. Dressed thus I was ready. I took the telescope, inside my jacket.

I followed their route at first, keeping near to the sea. There was no one else walking on the shore, but ahead of me four men were pulling in a long net, a new one, lemon-colored. They had the net almost in, most of it lying piled in a glinting froth beside them, but the catch was still in the shallow water—I could see the swarming gleams of the mackerel as the net came in hand over hand, the men uttering with each heave a single gutteral exclamation which carried clearly to me. I had no wish to approach too near them, even thus disguised, so I went up behind, onto the upper shore, where a sandy track goes through lavender and tamarisk, rising gradually away from the sea. The town was behind me now. Only a few scattered *chardaks* on the hillsides. There would be people up there, on the rocky terraces, working on their holdings. But at this distance, dressed thus, I would be simply an anonymous passer-by.

I had walked some two kilometers and was feeling tired already with the unaccustomed exercise, fully aware of my folly by this time, but obsessively unable to turn back. Then I saw the horses. They were tethered below me on a level bit of the foreshore, just above the jumble of rocks that cuts the headland off from any approach on foot from this side. There must at one time have been a massive fall of rock here. The sea has licked the rocks smooth, and in their reclinations they enclose pools, some of them deep, quite screened off from the land. Lydia and Mister Bowles would be down there, among the rocks.

I stood there looking down, concealed among the tamarisk. The sun had freed itself from its bands of mist, given way to brilliant incontinence. There was a great glittering track over the sea. Everything was as it should be at that hour, white stones of the shore, pale thrift among the stones, plumes of the tamarisk flower, sun-warmed scents of cistus and thyme. Silent among it all, somewhere down there, Lydia and Mister Bowles.

I thought I saw a flash of white, clothing or flesh. I took out my telescope and focused it. The boulders revealed their pockmarks and blemishes, encrustations that looked like rust or faded blood. Improbably fronded vegetation trembled with my trembling hands. Menacing, I always feel, things brought so near to the human eye. As if they resented it. Quite visible now the gleam and slide of water among the dark rocks. Nothing more than this for some time. Then, with hallucinatory suddenness and distinctness a bare brown arm whisked into the arbitrary frame of the lens, a thin brown arm with a gold circle at the wrist: Lydia's. In a second it is gone again. She is naked, they are swimming naked together. I picture their limbs below the surface, glimmering, his golden pale, hers darker, the slow refractions of their bodies, touching, coiling in the blue water. Nothing now but the speckling of long dead crustaceans, rust of algae on the higher surfaces of the rocks. Then, lower down, for no more than five seconds, I see them together, the shine of the man's vertebrae, her right shoulder, the soft fold of flesh below the armpit. Gone again.

Nothing more, I saw nothing more, Excellency, but I knew, with immediate sick excitement, what they would be doing there, on the warm shingle, between rock and water, in the glory of the early sun. I saw with my famous imagination every move they made there, I was aware, while I continued to hold the telescope, continued to hold things closer in pulsing violation of natural law, aware of everything they did to each other, I was both of them in conjunction, he and she giving and receiving in my own person what they gave and received, and for a moment or two I experienced marvelous serenity at this equipoise of being, a glimpse of paradise. Then the excitement returned, my own poor flesh stirred, demanded, my hands began to tremble violently. I could no longer hold the telescope. Even now, Excellency, that heat returns to me, that helpless stirring, even after my visit to Ali (which I am coming to shortly).

Let me say in extenuation that this was no common lust. Lydia, so long the compliant partner of my fantasy, Mister Bowles, with whom I had felt from the beginning such strong affinity . . . There was something, some element of beauty, of benediction, in what I felt. If, through the force of imagination, I had been able to go step by step with them to the culminating moment, would not my experience have been indistinguishable from his, from *theirs*?

But I could endure it no longer. I scrambled to my feet, clutching the wretched telescope, turned away from that silence among the rocks, and from the horses patiently cropping. Home, in my shuffling heelless shoes. Home, but the familiarity of my room failed to quiet me. I could, it is true, have ministered to myself, been my own subject and agent; it would not have been the first time my room had been witness to such *splendeurs et misères*, and on this occasion it would have been apt, almost poetic; but I needed another, Excellency, needed some touch that was not my own. Needed Ali, in short.

I changed into my linen suit, noticing as I did so that there were oil marks on the right lapel. Brown-and-white shoes, straw hat. The sun was higher now, it was beginning to be hot. I kept my head down, looked at no one, exchanged no greetings. Always now, when I go into the town, among the people, I am afraid. A glance misinterpreted, the wrong inflection in a greeting, anything now could be the death of me. I thought I heard a man hiss from a doorway, but I did not look.

The baths are in the *Konak*, an area of small shops, soup

kitchens, kebab stalls, where small traders, day-laborers and artisans live—Turk, Greek, Armenian and Jew living together in conditions of promiscuity and squalor. Effluvium from the houses runs down the open gutters of the sloping streets. Smells of urine, jasmine, burnt charcoal. Smells of my fortnightly indulgence, which I am now, under stress, anticipating by a few days. Today a sharper, more pervasive smell, noticeable here because of the airless closeness of the streets: the fetid smell of captive sheep. Silent now, however, in the heat, listless.

Past the mosque. Down the alley. A thin cat avoids me. The entrance is in the alley, between two streets. Five minutes later I am in my bath. Everything now inflames my need, every familiar sight and sound, beading of steam on the tiles, click of bath slippers on the boards, the coarse white towel on my rail. Bath, steam room, and at last the massage parlor. A private cubicle, *bien entendu*.

Ali shows rose-pink underlip in a smile of greeting. "*Merhaba effendim*," he says. "This is not your usual day." He notices everything.

"I could not wait," I tell him, and he smiles again. Ali is always very cheerful. He is cream-coffee-colored, the product of an irregular and probably forcible union of Arab father and Negro mother. From Mersin. He was a ship's boy, and stopped off here to escape a brutal and lascivious captain. He thinks he is fifteen. One day he intends to open his own steam bath and massage parlor, and he is grateful for the little extra money that I and my like give him for his special attentions. Ali will go far, I think. He has a marvelous understanding of the needs of the flesh.

I lie supine on the narrow bench, in total nudity save for the customary towel over the loins. His strong fingers knead the last cramp out of my limbs, work in the cool oil. When I am completely relaxed, almost swooningly passive, the towel of my modesty is gently removed and his hands touch me with intimate knowledge and skill. Touch by touch, with patient judgment, he takes me to the brim, dallies exquisitely with me in this state until my whole body is pleading, then brings me over to spill in protracted throbs and shudders, back to drained peace, acquiescence in man's miserable lot.

I know that by these confessions I will have increased your contempt for me. But they are connected, they are necessary. Besides, you need contempt to sustain your position. God is fed on contempt, they say.

That was, as I say, earlier today. Back in my room I found a note under the door from Mister Bowles, who had called in my absence. He wants me to arrange a further interview with Mahmoud Pasha, though he did not say why.

I was prey for some time to feelings of depression. Partly no doubt due to the hollowing of my being I had experienced under Ali's hands. *Triste omne animal.* Though this had not been exactly coitus. Then I was conscious of having spent rather a lot while it was still so early in the month. And of course, the blank, tyrannical pages there before me, still waiting to be filled. There is the isolation I live in, the end of my usefulness as an informer, the prefiguring of my death I see in the closed faces of those around me. I find some consolation in Schopenhauer, in his words about the indestructibility of being. No doubt your Excellency is acquainted with them. "This present moment, the sole form of reality, has its source within us, not without . . . Although when we die the objective world will be lost to us, as will the intellect with which we acknowledge that world, yet our existence will not be affected . . ."

If only I could picture existence without the world. I must try to sleep for an hour, or at least rest my eyes. Then it will be time to keep my rendezvous with Mrs. Marchant.

Excellency, a most extraordinary thing happened in the church tonight, which I must relate to you in all its ugliness and absurdity, while it is still fresh in my mind. Our Saint Alexi fell down, collapsed, disintegrated in full gaze of the congregation; owing to the ineptitude of the decrepit priest, or so I suppose. And I was blamed for it!

I met Mrs. Marchant as arranged outside the Café Lykis, and we went together to the church. Well, in fact we went into the café first, because Mrs. Marchant suggested it and I could think of no pretext for avoiding it. Not that I minded the time with her, on the contrary, but it was unfortunate, because gallantry impelled me to pay, thus further depleting my resources—Mrs. Marchant, in addition to coffee, had a slice of chocolate gateau.

I learned that her husband had been dead for two years and she was now fulfilling a lifetime's ambition to travel. She seems genuine enough, and of course American ladies are freer and more independent than their European counterparts. She was wearing a gray silk dress with a lace collar and carrying a white handbag which I surmised was full of money.

We talked mainly about Mrs. Marchant's enthusiasm for the ancient Greek world, and how on this island she saw all around her evidences of an unbroken link with the past. "That sound I heard just now," she said, "on my way here —it was an octopus being beaten against a rock, the man was just whipping the rock with it, over and over again. Why do they do that, by the way?"

"To make the meat tender," I said.

"Oh yes, they eat them, don't they? Well, that sound is the self-same sound they must have been hearing on this island for literally centuries. Don't you think that's wonderful?"

I answered this as best I could. Then I told her something about the ceremony we were about to see. Saint Alexi, I told her, was a man of very holy life and gifted with miraculous powers. He was in his youth dissolute and of loose morals, but underwent conversion near a village well in the interior, and thereafter spent his life in fasting and prayer, living apart from others in a cave not far from the place of his conversion. One day he vanished from there, and was never seen again by mortal eye. Or so it is said. It is believed that he was taken up to heaven. The well, though now dry, is still regarded as a holy place by the people of the island, and it is visited at certain times of the year, and votive offerings left there. In fact most of the stories about the saint relate to his powers of divining water, and his name is often invoked when there is danger of drought. Every year on this day his Assumption is enacted in the church of Aghios Giorgos on the outskirts of the town, a walk of about half a mile from where we were sitting.

Mrs. Marchant listened. She expressed herself as eager to see it all. The light was fading when we left the café. We walked through the streets together and Mrs. Marchant remarked on the quantity of flat unleavened loaves in some of the shops. I explained that it was the custom, among Moslems, to eat such bread at the time of the Sacrifice *Bayram*. I also pointed out to her the number of little stalls offering knives and cleavers for sale. She was struck by the great variety of these as to size and shape. I told her that they were for the cutting of the sheeps' throats. Knifemakers do a great trade during this *Bayram* because the Turks, though possessing knives already, feel impelled to buy some new cutting weapon at this time of the year. Rather in the same way, I said, as you might buy a new dress for a party.

"I see, yes," Mrs. Marchant said. However, her interest in local customs, hitherto so determined, seemed to falter a little at this point. "Perhaps," she said, after a pause, and without much conviction, "a new knife gives them a specially reverent sacrificial feeling?"

I agreed that this might be so. As you can imagine, Excellency, I did not feel very comfortable during this conversation. My own voice began to sound in my ears like a sacrificial bleat. In order to change the subject I pointed out to her the long crest of Mt. Leros, which the Turks call Alti Dag, that fluid line which God made with his finger in a moment of joy, the Greeks say. The rose-gold suffusions of sunset were ebbing from the crest, warmth and color fading from moment to moment, as from the rim of a broad crucible—the alchemical process reversed, gold into baser metal.

The church is built on a rocky eminence, behind the town and somewhat above it. A good number of people were going in the same direction as we were, the women in black, the men with clean shirts buttoned up to the neck. There were some sidelong glances, but nobody appeared to take much notice of us—rather surprisingly, I thought. Lamps had been hung along the way, and lamplight fell on the thick, pale blades of cactus that grew beside the steps. Above us, the church bells had started ringing. We stopped once, halfway up, to look back at the town. The white walls of the houses had on them the bloom of dying light, a kind of incandescence. Beyond them the sea lay glimmering and still. Far out in the bay a cluster of pale red lights—lanterns of fishing boats working their circular entrapment.

We went on to the top of the steps. The bells stopped abruptly and we heard chanting. The church was already full, but people stood aside for the foreign woman, and so we were able to get near the front. Here, in this public place, surrounded by Greeks, exposed and vulnerable, I felt a return of that exhilaration I had experienced with Dranas, Excellency. I had an urge to stand before them, declare myself. Fortunately for the rest of this report I did not do so. (Indeed, as you will see, I gave way to craven fear not long after.)

The litter stood at the top of the nave, just below the chancel, with the effigy of the saint lying on it, dressed still in his gold vestments. The lamps burning at the four corners threw light onto his sharp chin, and the holes of his nostrils. I recognized these features as I would those of an old acquaintance—after all, I have seen him thus often before. In his composure he looks corpselike indeed. The priests are intoning, one on either side of him and one beyond.

"It is very lifelike, isn't it?" Mrs. Marchant whispers to me. She means deathlike I think, really. She seems troubled. Disturbed perhaps in her reticent Protestantism, that so much more abstract religion. It is rather strong stuff for her, the incessant deep incantation, the wavering light of the candles playing on the gilt of the bier, the saint's waxen immobility, which expresses nothing of martyrdom, no hint of violence or wounds: nothing but death.

The crowd maintains an unbroken silence. Their faces are heavy and sad, their hands thick, clumsy-looking. They seem to be waiting for something other than the apotheosis of Alexi. The priests' chanting grows louder. Their vestments, faces, and hands are devotional and powerful in the gloom. Four men from the congregation move forward, all men I know. They take up the bier and move with it up the steps, into the chancel. They deposit it there and file down again, into the body of the congregation. The priests go slowly up the steps, still chanting. They pass into the chancel, drawing behind them a white curtain which shuts them off from the view of the people. The chanting ceases. All eyes are fixed on the curtain, behind which the priests are busy stripping the saint of his panoply, dressing the attenuated form in its Assumption robe, getting it to its feet. For some moments more there is silence, deep, expectant. Then a quick, running peal of bells. The curtain is drawn back, and the saint, in a blaze of light from the altar candles, stands upright before the congregation, dressed now in his long white robe. How the priests manage this bit of stagecraft, how they get the saint to stand on his own feet, so to speak, I have never discovered. Perhaps his feet are weighted, or some wedge is used, concealed by the robe. Whatever the method, Excellency, on this occasion something went badly wrong.

For some seconds he stood there. Long enough for the singing to recommence. Long enough for us all to meet his staring brown eyes and see the gleam on his features, like death-sweat. Then, very slowly at first, he began to keel over. One side of him seemed to be unsecured, so that he fell slightly sideways, with a strange effect of deliberateness, as if he had himself chosen the angle. One of the priests, with swifter reflexes than the others, stepped forward and made an attempt to catch the toppling saint, but the bier was in his way, and he was not quick enough. In the full blaze of altar lights, the cynosure of eyes, Saint Alexi, O *Alexi mas*, as the local people call him, our Alexi, went thudding down on his face, and—here is the crowning disaster, Excellency, if you will forgive the bad pun—on impact with the stone of the chancel floor his head came off altogether, snapped off clean at the neck, and went rolling down the steps, almost reaching the front ranks of the congregation. His headless form remained at the top, draped in its Assumption robe.

The singing had faltered, died away. There was a hush of consternation. I heard Mrs. Marchant say something in abrupt exclamation at my side, and felt her take my arm. Then those immediately around me, men and women, turned and looked at me, and there was the same expression on every face: not accusation, but *knowledge*, the final knowledge of some utterly detestable creature. I thought I saw relief there too, as if this was what they had really been waiting for. Several people made the sign of the cross. They blamed me for the debacle, Excellency. Now my treachery was confirmed. I was in the pay of the Turk and in league with the Devil. From spy to evil eye, a short step for these people. A man standing close by me—one Trikiriotis by name—suddenly stretched out his arm toward me, the fingers splayed and rigid. This is the curse on the five senses, Excellency. Others followed suit. I lost my nerve. I thought they were going to kill me. I turned, shaking myself free of

Mrs. Marchant, leaving her, unforgivably, alone and unprotected, and plunged blindly through the crowd. Somehow they parted for me. I rushed out of the church, down the steps, stumbling in my haste and panic, and so home.

That was some hours ago, Excellency. I have just opened my shutters. It is morning now. The sun has not risen yet, but there are preliminary stains on the sea. Setting all this down has calmed my fear, leaving me with a certain kind of resignation. Nothing really matters to me now but this report; and this report depends for balance and completeness, poignancy and point, on Mister Bowles. I knew that, from the beginning. Hence my efforts to make him real to your Excellency, to bring him before your eyes. And yet I cannot be sure that I have succeeded. His face is present now to my mind: narrow, long-jawed, with its reddish tan and the pale indignant eyes; the moustache, the smooth brown hair. Once again I am troubled by suspicions of him, by my sense of some discrepancy which I cannot define. I saw no books in his luggage. A man so interested in the past would carry books, surely, works of reference. Of course, there was the other bag, the one I was not able to examine; perhaps in there . . . My report began with him, he brought with him the taste of death, which has been in my mouth ever since. It must end with him, too. The thought of dying with my report unfinished, of leaving Mister Bowles to pursue his destiny unregistered and unrecorded, is a very bitter one.

I slept till noon, Excellency, then ate the bread and the peaches I bought yesterday. Peaches are plentiful this year and now is the time for them.

In the afternoon, in obedience to Mister Bowles's instructions, I went once more to see Izzet. I told him of the Englishman's request for a further meeting with the Pasha. He was curious, but I could tell him nothing. He said he would try to arrange matters for later today. So far I have heard nothing from him.

On the way back a rather odd thing happened. I ran into

Politis, the cotton merchant, at the corner of Paradisos, and instead of ignoring me, as I had expected, he smiled and paused. "You did not speak to us the other evening," he said.

"Speak to you?" I said. I was bewildered. They had failed to speak to *me*, Excellency.

"Yes," he said. "At the Metropole. Now you have more important friends, eh?"

"No, not at all," I said. "Any time . . . I would be glad—"

But Politis moved away, still smiling. Does he mean to be friendly? Could I possibly have been mistaken? If about him, then about all the others. No, impossible. It is a trick, a device to allay my suspicions until they are ready to act. A clever move, but it will not succeed. I will not be lulled.

Below me, some distance along the shore, a group of young men. Two of them wrestling, Turkish-style, stripped to the waist. Higher up, where it is sandy. Too far to distinguish faces. Laborers, judging by the sun-darkened forearms and necks. I watched them for some time, locked together, shifting and heaving, neither of them able to get the advantage. Again the equipoise, Excellency—God continues to pay me with symbols for my attention to this visible world.

Beyond them the sea, pale in the shallows, deepening in color as the water deepened, to a cobalt so intense the eye could not stay on it, was forced away, back to the softer hues of the shore, to the locked forms of the young men. Suddenly both fell heavily together onto the sand, extricated themselves there. When they got up, the game was different. Now one of them made stabbing motions toward the other. He had what looked like a piece of stick in his hand. He was simulating a knife or bayonet attack, and the other was warding off, evading, seeking to disarm. Their quickness and agility were impressive. Elemental too the postures of attack and defense, against the background of sea and rock.

Everywhere, in small things and in great, the world is rehearsing for violence, Excellency. Games on the beach, articles in newspapers, any casual conversation, all show the same impatience with peace. I saw it on the faces of people in church last night, mute, sad, a slow rage at inactivity— then the relief, the joy of hate, with which they turned to me. Everywhere a rising need for the gesture that shatters the glass.

Revelations, Excellency. I have just returned from the meeting with Mahmoud Pasha that Mister Bowles requested —it was not until this morning that we were able to go. Revelations. But I must get things in their proper order, must not allow Mister Bowles's amazing duplicity to throw my narrative into disarray. He is a trickster, Excellency.

He had the brown leather bag with him this time—the one I had seen him carrying when he descended from the ship. Worn, but of good quality. Of the type known as a Gladstone bag, I believe. I was curious about the reasons for this appointment and tried by various hints to draw Mister Bowles out, but he was obviously unwilling to discuss it. I did not tell him of Herr Gesing's warning, thinking it more to my advantage to keep quiet for the time being.

The sentry offered no hindrance to our passing. The parade ground, as before, was empty. We were met by an orderly, who showed us into the house—not this time into the reception room where we had been before, but into a much smaller room with a large desk, on which papers were scattered, and several upright chairs against the wall. There was no one here. The orderly asked us to wait. He seemed disconcerted at finding the room empty. He hesitated for some time at the door, then he went off down the passage, presumably to find some superior.

Mister Bowles and I had seated ourselves against the wall. But after a moment I got up again, moved casually over to the desk, and began glancing at the papers lying on it. I could feel his unspoken disapproval behind me—this was not the behavior of a gentleman. However, I persisted. I have my own code of practice, and the acquiring of information ranks high in it.

There was not much of interest among the papers. Official correspondence for the most part, addressed to Mahmoud Pasha, some of it dating from several months previously. It was obvious that the Commandant had no system for dealing with his letters. One I noticed because it bore the imperial seal, and contained a reference to a presumably German firm, *Mannfeldt GmbH*, also the phrase "terra rossa," which my eye hastily lighted on in the midst of the Turkish words. Beyond this was a map, a large-scale map with various marks on it in red ink. It was a local map, I realized after a moment: there was the line of Mt. Leros, with the whole line of the coast on that side of the island, including the area containing Mister Bowles's temporarily acquired domain.

Mister Bowles coughed, I think to denote disapproval. At that moment I caught some flicker of movement outside. I glanced through the small window and was in time to see the figures of Mahmoud Pasha and Herr Gesing walking side by side, in a direction away from me, the former in uniform, the latter black-suited. They were talking but not, it seemed to me, very amicably. In a moment more they had disappeared round the side of the house. Herr Gesing speaks Turkish, then—he has never admitted as much to me. Presumably taking his leave. I wonder what business brought him. On our previous visit, too, his name occurred, if you remember, Excellency.

I had only a few seconds more to look at the map; time enough, however, to see that a rough diamond shape had been traced out on it in red. Lying horizontally, its eastern point began just above the ancient harbor.

I heard steps outside the door, Izzet's voice raised in anger. Instantly I moved away from the desk, and took up a position near the window—there was no time to regain my seat. I think Izzet was upbraiding the orderly for leaving us alone. A moment later he entered, looking not exactly flustered, but certainly less than calm. "Please be seated," he said, giving me a sharp glance. He went to the desk and looked over it quickly, but without touching anything.

Mahmoud Pasha entered, his bulk encased in dark blue dress uniform with silver brocade on epaulettes and sleeves. His face was dark red, congested-looking. Again I had the feeling that the interview with Herr Gesing had not been a friendly one.

When we were again seated, Izzet and Mahmoud Pasha looked in expectant silence at Mister Bowles. There was a short, uneasy pause, then Mister Bowles, in his usual plunging way, said, "Well, the fact is, you'd better tell them I have found some objects on the site."

"Objects?" I said.

"What does he say?" Izzet pointed his nose at me.

"On the site they leased to me." Mister Bowles put one hand up, briefly, to his tie, and touched the knot. "They are of considerable archeological importance," he said. "There's a lot of stuff there."

"What does he say?" Izzet's thin lips twisted. He was getting impatient.

"He has found certain objects in the course of his researches." I said.

"What kind of objects?"

Mister Bowles leaned forward earnestly. "It is an important discovery," he said. "The point is that I want to ask them to change the lease so I can have the right to excavate the site. Of course I am willing to pay more for it—whatever they think fit."

Inwardly marveling, outwardly impassive, I translated this.

"*Valuable* objects?" Izzet said.

"He asks if they are valuable," I said.

"Yes, I suppose so," Mister Bowles said. "It depends on the material. Of course I shan't know what there is until I start digging."

For an appreciable period after this no one said anything at all, and this I could well understand. The blinding correctness of Mister Bowles's behavior was dazing them, as it had dazed me. He sat there before us, with his bag beside his chair, like a marvelous monster of rectitude. ·

"*Large* objects?" Izzet said at last. "*Buyuk dir?*" A natural question. If they were large, of course, it would go some way toward making Mister Bowles's behavior human and explicable: large objects could not be pocketed, removed surreptitiously—time was needed.

"I have them here in my bag," Mister Bowles said.

"Small objects apparently," I said to Izzet. "He has them in his bag."

The eyes of both Izzet and the Pasha leaped at once to the bag.

"I would be willing to double the sum," Mister Bowles said.

I translated this.

Mahmoud Pasha shifted his bulk behind the desk, and his chair winced. "Let us see the objects," he said. His eyes were still on the bag.

Without waiting for me to translate this, Mister Bowles began to unbuckle the side straps of his bag. It seemed to take a long time. Finally, when the brass clasp at the top had also been undone, he opened the bag. Then he paused again, surely with a showman's instinct, and said, "Perhaps I could put the objects on your desk?"

"Certainly," the Pasha said. "*Buyurun.*" I had never seen him look so alert and generally *exhypnos*.

Mister Bowles got up rather awkwardly, still holding the open bag. He moved over to the desk. His hand went into the bag and emerged, holding something. The others were looking only at his hands, but I glanced up at his face, and saw him lick his lips in two quick movements of the tongue. He placed the object on the desk.

It was the marble head of a woman, pale honey-colored, the size of a smallish human fist. And I had seen it before.

Recognition was not immediate, did not come flooding into my mind, but was achieved in a series of incredulous stabs, or pangs. The head seemed to palpitate, so intently did I eye it. But of course there was no doubt: it was the same head.

"I think this is the most interesting of the finds to date,"

Mister Bowles said. After that small betraying movement of the tongue, his face was quite calm again. "I thought at first it was Roman," he said to the red-faced and astounded Mahmoud Pasha. "A Roman copy, you know. But the workmanship is extremely delicate, particularly in the treatment of the hair. I think it is Hellenistic work, almost certainly from the corner of a sarcophagus."

With the same feeling of incredulity I heard my voice translating, purveying information about this head for the benefit of Mahmoud Pasha and Izzet; this head I had seen in his room on the evening of his arrival, before he had so much as left the hotel; this head he had undoubtedly brought with him to the island.

"Early third century B.C." Mister Bowles said, with what seemed genuine interest and pleasure. "And look at the marble." He picked the head up and displayed it to us. "That is not local marble," he said.

I glanced at Mahmoud Pasha and Izzet. It was obvious that neither of them was at all interested in what the Englishman was saying. This lump of marble must have come as a distinct anticlimax.

"It is Pendelic marble," Mister Bowles said, "and you know what that means, of course. Then there is this. This is quite a different kind of object." His hand was in his bag again. His voice, I noticed now, was calmer, more deliberate in falsehood than in the blurts of his everyday speech. "Less interesting perhaps than the head," he said.

He laid on the table, alongside the head, a thick circlet of metal, in which were set blue stones. The metal had a yellowish gleam. "Roughly the same period, I should say," he said. "I have a theory about these things, actually."

"He says it belongs to the same period," I said, abetting Mister Bowles in the absurd pretense that Izzet and the Pasha were interested in the historical aspect. The circlet I had not seen before.

Mahmoud Pasha picked it up, looked at it against the light, weighed it in his palm. "*Alti*" he said. "It is gold." His voice sounded changed to me, everything seemed changed, voices, light, above all Mister Bowles, standing upright before the desk—by "upright" I am describing only his posture, Excellency, not his character as I now viewed it.

"The *Vali* remarks that it is gold," I said.

"Oh, yes, it's gold all right," Mister Bowles said, with studious seriousness as if this mere utterance of avarice on the Pasha's part had been a contribution to the discussion about the date. "Yes, that is quite true, and I take your point that gold was not mined here, but the workmanship, you will notice, is Greek. These islands were importing gold from Africa in the third century. The stones, of course, are turquoises."

Clever of him to produce this valuable object only second, showing that his interests were scholarly, not grossly material; thus maintaining at these culminating moments the pose that had deceived us all.

Izzet Effendi leaned forward, passing a thin hand over his mouth and jaw. "Gold?" he said.

Mahmoud Pasha passed the circlet over to him and he peered closely at it for several moments with various exclamations of piety—his religious feelings roused by the sight of such wealth. He was making as if to pass it back to his overlord, but Mister Bowles politely intercepted it, laid it back on the table alongside the head. "Then there are these few things," he said, ferreting once more in his bag. He placed on the table various shards of pottery and a small terra cotta jar with a broken handle. "They were all together in the one place," he said. "Red-figured, the fragments. Corinthian, by the look of it."

This said, he returned quietly to his seat. There ensued a heavy silence among the four of us in that room. Mister Bowles looked politely at the window. Izzet and the Pasha looked at each other and at him. They were handicapped, of course, fatally handicapped from the start. A prospect of great wealth was being opened out before them, with dazing suddenness—if the Englishman were the mooncalf he seemed. And he *was*, he must be. Who but a mooncalf would have been willing to pay so much for the lease? And now, declaring his finds in this way . . . You begin to see, Excellency, the beauty of the conception?

"How did you find these objects?" Izzet wanted to know. He peered at Mister Bowles as if scenting carrion.

Mister Bowles explained, with my assistance, that he had been exploring the remains of the Roman villa up there, that he had in his scrambling happened to dislodge some loose stones and rubble immediately below the arch of the doorway—there was only this one arch left standing. Perhaps they did not know, he said in parenthesis, that the Virgin Mary was said to have spent her last days here, after the death of Christ? He did not think this could be so, the villa being of too early a date, though it was possible, certainly it was possible. He had gone head over heels himself, he said. When he picked himself up he saw that the fall of stone had revealed a cavity in the hillside which narrowed into what looked like a vertical shaft, or perhaps part of another house, built lower down. He had not been able to explore this because of the danger of further landslides. But he had found the objects in question just inside the opening, lying all together.

"My theory is," said Mister Bowles, "that the villa was built on or near the site of an earlier house, by that time in ruins. They probably used the same foundations, without looking at what was underneath. There was a sanctuary to Artemis there from very early times. That argues a certain population. I think these objects are part of a collection formed by the owner of the earlier house, probably sometime during the period of the Attalids. Someone very wealthy. Perhaps from Ephesus or Bergama."

"And the rest of the collection?" Izzet said.

"I think it is there," Mister Bowles said, without a tremor. "There, underneath the villa, you know."

There was another, longish pause. Then Mister Bowles said, "Tell them I will double the money, if they will agree to let me excavate the site."

I put this offer to the Pasha, who rested for a full minute

in profound immobility. Then he said, "I wish to confer with my land agent. Will you wait outside for a little while?"

Mister Bowles sauntered casually to the table and slipped the circlet into his pocket. The other things he left there. Then we obediently filed out. We left them there together, Excellency. Mahmoud Pasha obese and torpid, Izzet delicate and peering. Turk and Arab—physically they could not have been more dissimilar, but the contrast was only superficial: they were two men in the toils of an identical dream.

They did not keep us waiting long. Standing at his desk the Pasha delivered the answer that I—and I am sure Mister Bowles too—had expected.

"We cannot extend the lease," he said.

"Amend," I said. "Not extend."

It was my care for words that led me to the foolishness of thus correcting him. He looked at me steadily and without expression for some moments. I felt a chill in the region of the spine. My superior vocabulary will not help me, if once I fall into his hands.

"Neither," Izzet said. "We can agree to neither. These objects are the property of the government."

Mister Bowles rose and moved with apparent casualness toward the desk. "I am aware of that," he said. "And I intend to see that they are handed over to the proper authorities in Constantinople." Without haste, watching Izzet and Mahmoud steadily, he returned the objects to the depths of his bag, adding to them the circlet from his pocket. He used only his left hand for this. The right remained by his side. "I shall see to it personally," he said. "As I am sure you know, a collection is currently being formed by the Ministry at Gulhane, as the nucleus of a National Museum."

I translated these remarks to them, watching as I did so Mister Bowles take up the bag, again using only his left hand. The right remained by his side, hanging loosely, fingers open. I glanced round the room for places of cover, but saw none.

"Has he told anyone else of this?" Izzet said.

No, it appeared that he hadn't.

"And the papers, has he them with him?" Izzet looked quickly at his master. "Perhaps," he said, "if we could see the papers . . ."

Mister Bowles's blue gaze was expectantly on me. I felt the perspiration break out on my body. If once they got their hands on the papers it would be all up with us.

"They want to know if you have the documents with you," I said. "For God's sake, say no."

"You can tell them," he said, very coldly, "that the contract and the receipt are deposited under seal, with instructions for forwarding, in the event of my non-return, to the British Consul at Smyrna. Together with a note setting out the circumstances."

I should have known, of course, that he would not fall into such a trap. Not the man before me, with his hand ready by his side. The trouble was that I was still seeing him partly as the victim, the dupe—so strong had been that earlier impression of his simplicity.

"He will never get a permit," Izzet said. "It would need a firman, from Constantinople. That would take longer than three weeks. The lease will have expired."

"In that case, I will simply have to report my discoveries to the Ministry," Mister Bowles said. "They will do the excavating, I suppose. A pity, because I should have liked my name to be associated with the discoveries, especially if they turn out—and I think they will—to be of first importance."

"The lease must revert to us," Izzet said. His eyes were moist with rage.

"But it has three weeks to run," I said. In spite of my fear some relish at their discomfiture must have showed in my voice, because Izzet looked at me with sudden intensity. "You," he said, "I advise you to be careful."

"The land is my property," the Pasha said, and his voice was thick with contempt for the foreigner, contempt for all restriction, law and limit. "My property," he repeated. He raised one heavy hand and loosened his tunic at the neck. A vein had become prominent at his temple.

Still holding the bag in his left hand, Mister Bowles moved toward the door, keeping them both within his sight. I rose with alacrity and followed. He was at the door when Izzet spoke.

"We will buy it back," Izzet said. "We will buy back the lease from you."

"They say they will buy it." I was translating quite mechanically—past all astonishment now.

"Buy it?" Mister Bowles paused, as if this was quite a new idea. "I dare say they want to see their names associated with the exhibits when they appear in the new museum at Gulhane," he said. "Well, it's natural, I suppose."

I translated this.

"Yes, yes," Izzet said eagerly. "That is the reason."

"Well, now," Mister Bowles said. "This puts a new slant on things, you know. Naturally, in view of the inconvenience, the disruption to my research and so on, I should have to ask rather more than I gave. I think seven hundred liras would be a fair figure."

Seven hundred liras, Excellency. That is a good sum of money, even in these days. It is considerably more than my yearly income. I saw Izzet's eyelids fluttering.

"They have till noon tomorrow," Mister Bowles said. "I will wait at my hotel."

We left them sitting there. No move was made to hinder our departure, no sound came after us. In the *fiacre*, on the way back, neither of us said much. Once or twice, at the beginning, Mister Bowles breathed deeply and audibly, the only sign of tension that he showed. Once I saw a smile on his face. I myself was silent. Vistas were opening before me, a way at last of breaking out. I was content to wait, plan my tactics. I have him in the hollow of my hand, Excellency.

I HAVE SLEPT, waked, slept again—both sleep and waking filled with the wondrous events of yesterday. Early still—the dawn prayer has just sounded. Hot already, and absolutely still. The *imbat* which has been troubling us lately has dropped. Striations of light across the sea, paling with distance, continuing into the long motionless plumes of cloud on the horizon. The verge so ethereal that cloud above seems denser, like further masses of land. Then the true land, the shapes of islands, glimpsed beyond. Layer upon layer, zone upon zone. Most beautiful and bewildering—liquid and solid, reality and illusion, form and light all confounded.

Through these soft distances, as it were through the hems of light, I hear the cries of sheep. The slaughter has begun. Today is the tenth day of *Zilhijje*. Throughout your possessions, Excellency, wherever the green flag of the Prophet is flown, they will be sharpening their knives. Thousands upon thousands of beasts bleeding their lives into the earth, their heads held toward Mecca. Killed soberly, in the Turkish fashion.

Today too—and now I am making your Excellency privy to my criminal projects—today I intend to extort money from Mister Bowles. Did I not say at the outset that I would hide nothing from you? I must have money, my life is impossible here. I must get to Constantinople, make full inquiry into the neglect of my reports . . .

When I saw him lay the head on the desk, after the first shock at his perfidy, my real, my overwhelming feeling was one of identity with him. No, more intimate than that. An effect of *fusion*. I remember again Herr Gesing's hands locked together. *Eng verbunden*. Artist and trickster. I know Bowles despises me, has done so from the very start. But it is the me in him that he despises. Adepts both at the partial lie, blends of reality and illusion. Now I understand better my distress when I saw him sporting with Lydia. Mister Bowles produced a real head in an imaginary setting. What more can art do?

Think of the beauty of the idea, Excellency. Everything he has done, everything he has said, has been essential to his effect. No gesture has been superfluous. No doubt afar off he got wind of things here, a whiff of the pickings, so to speak. He must have arrived with the project already formed in his mind—with some room for improvisation, of course. Never was there wolf in better tailored sheep's clothing. Touch by touch he created himself for us, allowed us to create him, an image of forthrightness and simple decency. The disapproval with which he greeted my chatter about my poor mother, the crashing rectitude of the sentiments he expressed to Herr Gesing about morality in politics, his ethical approach to painting—all part of his design.

Seeing so quickly the use he could make of me was perhaps the most brilliant part of his whole campaign. He had recognized my corruption at once—seen himself in me, Excellency, though despising it. It was a *faiblesse* that made me the perfect agent for dealing with people like Izzet and Mahmoud Pasha. Subtle enough, crooked enough, to convince men so dishonest of his total honesty.

And they, what can they do? Publicity of any kind would be the death of their hopes. They dare not leave him long on the site. They can neither act against him, nor wait. All they can do is pay.

ㅤ

Excellency, since I wrote those last words, not more than three hours ago, I have got onto a new footing with Mister Bowles; our relationship has changed greatly. I am now, up to a point, his partner in this enterprise. One hundred and fifty liras is promised me, more money than I have ever had in my possession. I shall save my skin, get off the island. Not only that. The money will be sufficient for me to stay in Constantinople, find out—at last—what has been happening to my reports. It is many years since I felt such joy, Excellency, such pure joy.

Izzet came punctually to the hotel. We sat amid the potted palms, beneath the scenes of Zeus's loves, in the otherwise deserted lounge. The abundant charms of the nymphs above his head made Izzet, in fez and alpaca jacket, seem even more shrunken and diminutive than usual. After the usual polite preliminaries, Izzet offered to buy back the lease for double what Mister Bowles had paid—or not paid, rather, since in fact he has paid nothing so far but the ten liras deposit.

Mister Bowles rejected this offer very firmly. "That just isn't good enough," he said. "They really cannot expect me to . . ." His blue eyes full of expostulation, a note of strong indignation in his voice. "My research," he said. "The whole progress of my book has been held up. And then, you know, there is the disappointment . . . I mean, I should have liked my name to be associated with these finds. They could affect our knowledge of the whole period."

Had I not known the truth I would have sworn he was in earnest. There was a blaze of true feeling, true injury in his tone, in his whole manner. Obviously he is a perfectionist, a true artist, allowing no vulgar admixture of triumph or cynicism, even in these crowning moments. Or, the disturbing suspicion came to me as I watched his face, could he be *serious*? Did he in some way believe what he was saying?

"No, my dear chap," he said. "I must have seven hundred liras, at least."

I was reassured, though not completely, by the exorbitance of his demand. As for Izzet, his eyelids fluttered with agitation. He stood up, as if to go. "How can I return with such an offer?" he said. "It is out of the question."

"Well," Mister Bowles told him, "that is my figure. And by the way," he added, as Izzet still hesitated, "I have been up there this morning and I see you have stationed two soldiers on the site."

Izzet at once denied that he knew anything about this.

"Be that as it may," Mister Bowles said. "It is hardly a mark of trust, is it? There was nothing in our agreement about a military presence."

Izzet sat down again. He is highly strung and was quite distinctly trembling by this time. He looked like a vulture under powerful stress. "Tell him," he said to me, "that the *Vali* has authorized me to offer six hundred liras, but fifty liras must be deducted, because that is the used proportion of the lease. That is the final offer."

"Five hundred and fifty?" Mister Bowles reflected for a moment or two. Izzet saved what dignity he could by refraining from looking at the Englishman's face, or at mine. "Very well," Mister Bowles said. "I will accept that. It isn't enough, really, but I don't want to haggle."

"He agrees," I said. I did not translate the final remarks out of pity for Izzet.

"The money will be ready this evening," Izzet said.

"Shall we say seven o'clock, then? Good."

"The effendi will have the documents?"

"Oh yes," Mister Bowles said. "I'll have the documents all right."

"Until this evening then." Izzet departed, beneath the lofty gaze of the Prussian whoremaster.

"This calls for a drink," Mister Bowles said. He gave his slow smile, and his eyes widened, in that attractive combination of effects that was becoming familiar to me.

It was not a smile of triumph. There was nothing gloating about it. It seemed rather to express a kind of calm vindication, as if Mister Bowles had made a bold stand for truth and right, and been justified.

"One would almost say," I said, "that you had been through this kind of thing before."

He did not stop smiling, but he looked at me with a more particular attention. "Good heavens, no," he said. "Hardly the kind of thing . . . Why do you say that?"

"Oh, I don't know," I said. "The way you handled it. What about the soldiers?"

"Albanians, by the look of them. They are bivouacked up there, overlooking the site. They didn't lose much time, did they?" He paused. His face had suddenly assumed a look of indignation and contempt. "They're terrified that I'm going to cart the stuff off," he said.

"You wouldn't do that," I said.

"No, of course not. But you know what these people are like. How about a drink?"

I chose aniseed brandy again, again because of the *mezedes*. Mister Bowles asked for white wine.

"I am grateful to you for your help," he said. His eyes looked into mine directly, candidly. "When things are finally settled," he said, "I will see that you are not the loser by it."

The moment had come. We were sitting opposite each other, with only the narrow table between us. There were other people in the room now, but no one within earshot. Still I hesitated. I was afraid of him, physically afraid. Besides that, in a curious way I was in awe of him, because of his monumental hypocrisy. When people transgress violently against one's conception of them, Excellency, they assert themselves with peculiar vividness, they oblige us to look at them with washed eyes, so to speak. He was so far not what I had thought him that he awed me. Other pictures, former impressions, still clung to him, confusing my mind: the tall stranger momentarily bareheaded among the haggling Greeks, the amphibious lover, the conjuror with the Gladstone bag. His manner was the same as on the evening we met. He showed the same capacity for moral indignation, the same awkward bursts of speech. But it had all to be interpreted somehow differently now. I felt constrained, shy almost, as one would with a stranger.

I am aware that I am about to incriminate myself in your eyes. I should have reported Mister Bowles already. He has changed me. Today, *Kourban Bayram*, in the year of the Prophet 1286, sitting opposite Mister Bowles the trickster, aware of the commerce of the town proceeding outside, noting with approval that Biron has brought bread with the squid, I knew that this was a turning point in my life. My poor stratagems of the past paled before this one. And it was this knowledge that kept me still silent. I remarked on the heat. I mopped with monogrammed handkerchief the sides of my neck. I drank some of the water that had been brought with my aniseed brandy.

"These people," Mister Bowles said, and the contempt was back on his face and in his voice. "They are so absolutely, totally *mercenary*. There is no spark of . . . Well, I know it's an old-fashioned word these days, but there doesn't seem to be any concept of *honor* among them. It's no wonder the Ottoman Empire is breaking up, if what I've just seen is an example."

It was this piece of insolence that emboldened me, Excellency, drove me to speech. He was taking me for as great a fool as the others.

"That head," I said. "You brought it with you."

"I beg your pardon?"

I speared another pink crisp sliver of squid on my fork. My hands were unsteady. I am the most pacific of mortals, and Mister Bowles is a man acquainted with violence. "You brought it with you," I said. "You didn't find it here."

Our eyes met now, really I think for the first time fully, my solipsistic brown ones, his enterprising blue. Across the narrow table, across chasms of difference, I saw my image. Then with sudden shyness I glanced away. "You needn't keep up this pretense with me," I said.

"Pretense?" he said. "What are you talking about?" He had paled, or so I thought, under the tan, and I saw his chest move with the deep intake of his breath.

"That head," I said, "the head you produced from your bag, with the air of a conjuror if I may say so, that self-same head was in your possession when you set foot on this island, and so by inference were all the other objects which you laid on Mahmoud Pasha's desk."

I put down the fork and clasped my hands together under the table, in an effort to control their trembling. I kept my eyes away from Mister Bowles, I think out of some kind of tact—I was allowing him time to find a suitable face. When I did look his way again I found him regarding me closely.

"You must have a reason for saying this," he said.

I told him how I had found the head in his room that evening. Naturally I did not mention the revolver or notebook.

"What were you looking for?" he asked. "Are you a police agent?"

"I am nothing to do with the police."

"Some kind of informer, anyway," he said, with the same contempt.

I felt the blood rush to my face. It was not shame, Excellency—I am proud of my calling. It was partly that even now, perhaps particularly now, I wanted him to like me, to think well of me, and so I was wounded by his disparaging tone. But it was more than this. In those moments, as I paused before replying, all my frustration, all the pain of unjust neglect, rose up in me, led me to betray myself. In a voice I could barely control, I said, "No, not some kind— the best kind, I am the best kind."

"An informer," he said again.

"And you are a swindler," I said, trying to master my agitation, "and the laws against that kind of thing are severe in the domains of the Sultan, not to say savage. As in all societies where malpractices are rife. Not to mention the fact that a word from me would certainly be sufficient to spoil your game here, and lose you the money."

"Swindler?" he said. "You understand nothing about it. They have impeded my research."

It was astonishing; even in the rush of my feelings I was checked. He was the same, Excellency: the angry candor of those blue eyes, as if at some impatience with the world for failing to be adequate to his conception; honesty like a sort of suppressed rage in him; the halting yet curiously eloquent manner of his speech, with its awkward pauses and sudden blurts of assertion. It was difficult not to believe all this was genuine, even now.

"You understand nothing," he repeated. "I am simply an instrument."

I did not pay much attention to this remark at the time, being too eager to drive home my advantage. But I remembered it afterward, and his face saying it.

"At the moment," I went on, "time is working in your favor. Time and their greed and what they think of as your stupidity. They are obliged to gamble on your honesty—which I have helped you to establish. Any doubt of this and your scheme falls flat. And so do you. I want two hundred liras."

He was silent for a full minute. He looked briefly round the room, then his eyes returned to my face, steadied there, as if he was aiming. I did not like this look of his.

"Have you told anyone else?" he said. "About finding the head, I mean."

Fortunately I had anticipated this question. I had, in fact, learned from him. "No," I said, "but I have left a written account of everything from start to finish, in a sealed envelope, with forwarding instructions in the event of my disappearance or death."

"I very much doubt it," Mister Bowles said. "Still . . . I'll give you a hundred. You are entitled to something, anyway."

"A hundred and eighty," I said, with relief—while bargaining one is safe. "I won't take a piastre less."

We argued for some time with that spurious intimacy, a kind of imitation friendship, which such negotiations induce. In the end I exacted a promise of one hundred and fifty liras, contingent of course on the deal with Mahmoud Pasha going through. I promised in my turn to act as intermediary with Izzet this evening, when he comes with the money. And so we parted, he to retire to his room, I to make my way back here.

One hundred and fifty liras! I can hardly believe it. I shall get some new clothes in Constantinople. A couple of silk shirts, a new suit. Then, suitably dressed, I can make my approaches to your officials. A new pair of spectacles too.

My present ones do not suit my eyes, as I have explained, and besides the frame has been broken and repaired with wire, so they are unsightly in every sense. Once I have the money I can be on the next boat.

This report will be finished then, of course—my departure will bring it to a natural close. Mister Bowles too will be leaving, and the report has centered on him. This brings us to a very delicate juncture, Excellency. My whole situation has changed in the course of the last few hours, and our relationship, yours and mine, has changed with it. I have realized from the beginning that when you receive this report you will see that my usefulness is over. As an informer on this island I am finished. Moreover, in my rage for completeness, in my passion for your *acknowledgment,* I have revealed to you that on one level—though not the deepest—I have been falsifying my reports for many years. And now, by failing to report Mister Bowles, by turning the situation to my own advantage, I am compounding a felony. If these things became known to you, you would be displeased, you would have me arrested, all access to the archives would then be denied me.

I thought it didn't matter, you see. I thought my life was at an end. One final shape, as perfect as I could make it, wrought at the edge of the abyss, then my body toppling over. But everything is changed now, my life is opening up before me. Some small clerical post perhaps. My needs are few. The remaining years devoted to the collating and editing of my papers . . . You see how things are, Excellency, I cannot send you this report yet, if ever. For the moment I must simply shelve the question. Out of habit and piety I shall continue to address my words to you. And for the sake of unity of form, of course.

The smell of blood hangs over the island. On my way back I could smell it, thick and heavy in the midday heat. It seems to me that I can smell it still. Here and there blood-sodden patches on the roads. Below the marketplace a small group had gathered, among them children with round eyes. In their midst a sheep, mute, combed and dressed for death, horns gilded, fleece dyed red with henna. Twisted into the wool were amulets, ribbons, little colored streamers of paper. She stood for the last time on her four legs, head down, exhausted with terror. I hurried past, to avoid the sight of the killing. But I was helpless to avoid the picturing of it, saw them force the beast over, kneel on her to keep her down, turn her dyed head to the east; saw the cut, and the life-blood welling thickly out. Once the cut is made they die without a sound and without a struggle, eyes gently closing.

I was waiting for death like that sheep, until today. Red morocco and gilt lettering. Dedicated of course to you, Excellency.

H E DID NOT COME. He was not in his room, either. Izzet and I were there punctually at seven, but no Mister Bowles. Izzet had the money in a cloth bag, all ready to hand over. We sat there for ten minutes, making uneasy conversation. Then Mardosian approached us and handed me a sealed envelope. Nothing on the cover. Inside a note for me, very brief, without salutation. "Unavoidably detained," he said. "The troops are still on the site. Tell them I refuse to negotiate until these troops are removed. Tell them it is a matter of principle." Small neat writing. His signature at the end. I looked up dazed from this to meet Izzet's peering gaze. "He can't come," I said.

"Why not?"

"He doesn't say. He refuses to go on with the agreement until the soldiers are removed from the site."

"Allah, Allah," Izzet said, raising his hands. "What difference can that make now? He has nothing more to do on the site."

"He says it is a matter of principle."

"Principle?" Izzet rose abruptly. His face was bitter with rage. "*Shaitan* take his principles," he said. "And him, and you. He is playing games with us."

"I will see him," I said. "I will arrange another meeting."

"I advise you to be quick, *arkadeshim*. The *Vali* is not a patient man. It is on your head now."

"Yes," I said. "I will see to it." With anguish I watched him walk away, carrying my freedom in his bag. What can have happened? What bee has entered Mister Bowles's head? He did not seem to mind so much about the soldiers this morning. He made no conditions then.

All my hopes, Excellency. I can write no more tonight, my misery is too great. I must see Mister Bowles.

H E DID NOT RETURN to his hotel last night, or if so, it was very late. I waited, but he did not return. This morning, however, I have seen him. And I still cannot properly absorb what he said to me, the simple enormity of it. I sit here and look at the walls, my familiar possessions, with incredulity. I repeat his words to an imagined third party, trying to make them more accessible to the understanding. "I'd like to leave it for a day or two, old chap," was what he said. Nonchalantly. Leaning back in his chair. Right ankle laid over left knee, polished black shoe idly jigging. A day or two! This was in the little cafe-bar in Saliras Street, near the market.

It was by the merest chance that I was led to him. I knew he had not been back to the hotel. I was walking through the market when I saw three men at a fruit stall, men I had not seen before. I always pause to observe strangers; it is an ingrained habit with me.

I took them at first for Greeks, but there was something different about the way they carried themselves, and about their gestures. Besides this, one of them, while deeply tanned, had a lighter coloring than is customary in this region. He was a man of about forty, short but very powerfully built, wearing a blue calico jacket. There were gaps in his teeth when he smiled. The other two were indubitably men of the south, one elderly with a deeply seamed face and a gold ring in one ear, the other much younger, smooth-skinned and serious. I watched them buy aubergines and tomatoes, which the young man put into a cloth bag. Then after a brief conversation they separated, the thickset man walking off along Saliras Street, the other two moving slowly toward the steps that lead down to the lower part of the town.

After hesitating a moment I followed the man in the blue jacket, not too close, but keeping him well in sight. He walked down Saliras Street, almost to the end of it, then turned quickly into the little bar there, called the Agoraki. I had some idea of walking in after him, but fortunately stopped outside and looked through the window, standing against the wall at an angle that made it difficult for me to be seen. I did not see anything of the man I had followed except one of his blue sleeves and a brown hand on the table. But opposite him, full in my view, was Mister Bowles. He was talking, and I could imagine the pauses, the eloquent blurts. Excellency, he was not at the hotel last night, but he was fresh and clean-shaven. He looked like a man who had slept and breakfasted. I saw him raise his head and laugh.

I crossed the street and waited. After something like half an hour they emerged, shook hands briefly in the doorway under the blue awning, then went different ways, Mister Bowles toward the corner of the street, the other back toward the market. I watched him as he passed opposite to me. There was still some laughter in his face from the meeting. I noticed his belt, very broad with a heavy brass buckle in the shape of a snake.

Mister Bowles hesitated for a moment or two at the corner, as if making up his mind which way to go. I moved quickly along the street toward him, and called his name. He turned, saw me, and stood there waiting. He did not smile.

"What happened to you last night?" I said. I was panting slightly with the haste of my movements.

"I was held up," he said. "You got my note, I suppose?"

"Listen," I said, "I must talk to you."

He looked at me for a moment or two, then said, indifferently, "All right, if you like. I've got to meet Lydia and Mrs. Marchant in about an hour's time. Let's go over to the bar there." It was the one he had just come out of, but he didn't mention that.

It was cool inside, with the blinds down against the sun. We asked for a bottle of beer and two glasses. "Who was that man?" I said.

"Which man?"

"The one you were with just now. I saw you talking together."

"Did you? Oh, he was just someone I bumped into. Mrs. Marchant was telling us about that business in the church that other evening." He looked curiously at me. "Extraordinary," he said.

"You mean Saint Alexi biting the dust?" I said. "Yes, it was gruesome, his head went rolling down the steps. What nationality was he, by the way? The man you were talking to just now."

"Oh, American, I think. She says you ran off and left her."

"She was in no danger," I said. "None whatever."

"And you were?"

"Didn't she tell you how they all turned on me and started making the curse sign at me? They blamed me for it, you know, the accident."

He looked at me with a sort of faintly smiling curiosity.

"She says they were simply crossing themselves," he said.

"Nonsense," I said. "They were about to attack me."

Mister Bowles hitched his chair back, placed his right ankle over his left knee, and commenced a jigging motion with his shoe. This struck me as uncharacteristic of him, and made me more sharply aware of something I had sensed only half consciously since the beginning of our conversation, some difference in him, some quality of impatience or perhaps excitement that underlay the good-humored casualness of his manner.

"Listen," I said, "you realize, don't you, that they will be absolutely furious with us about last night? They are dangerous people. We must get the thing finished today, this morning."

Mister Bowles looked towards me without replying. His eyes were vague, remote, not really regarding me at all.

"We'll lose the money at this rate," I said, annoyed at being thus relegated to the margin of his attention. Annoyed too at my helpless sense of some change in him since our last meeting. "We'll lose the money and get our throats cut into the bargain," I said. "Don't make the mistake of assuming too much rationality in these people. If they suspect us of double-dealing—and they will, if we delay—they are quite capable of having us killed, whatever the consequences. Mahmoud would hope to cover it up, somehow. I know these people."

He went on jigging his shoe for a moment or two, then he said, quite casually, "I'd like to leave it for a day or two, old chap."

"Leave it?" I said. I was bewildered. "But why?"

"Well, you see, I haven't finished my research yet."

"Your research? But, please listen to me, time is everything in the matter. They are certain to suspect something."

"Suspect what?" he said, with assumed hauteur. "Didn't I make it clear to them that I am writing a book?"

"I don't know," I said. I was in despair, Excellency, close to tears. "I don't remember. What if you did? What is your book to them?"

"You thought the whole thing was a fabrication, I suppose?"

Once again, in spite of everything between us, and everything I know, he had me in the thrall of his outraged honesty. "Do you think," he said, "that I am going to let those people come between me and my research?"

My eyes were smarting with the effort to repress tears. My life, the money, everything falling away from me. "Why did you not make this clear before?" I said.

Mister Bowles saw my distress, I think, for his manner became gentler. "Listen," he said, leaning forward with one of his blurts of candor, "if it will set your mind at rest, you can give them my word."

"What?" I said.

"You can give them my word of honor that I will not remove any of the treasures on the site."

His word of honor. He looked at me, leaning forward still, with that engaging eagerness which was his great charm. The sense he conveyed was that we were partners in a great enterprise, something exciting and challenging and thoroughly worthwhile.

"But there are no treasures on the site," I said.

"True, of course that's true." He seemed momentarily disabled. "But they don't know that," he said, recovering. "They don't know that, do they? It'll only take a couple of days, you know."

"A couple of days," I repeated dully.

"That's all." He stood up. "Must be getting along," he said.

"The soldiers," I said, "have they been moved?"

"Oh yes," he said. "They're nowhere to be seen. Are you coming?"

"No, I don't think so." I was not eager to meet Mrs. Marchant again, and he knew it. He was smiling as he went out.

My God, what am I to do? What am I to do, Excellency?

I WENT TO SEE Doctor Hogan, the only person I could think of. Izzet caught me on the way back. It was only a question of time, I suppose. He was with another man.

Doctor Hogan's house is up above the town, on the hillside. It is a beautiful house, high-walled and shallow-roofed in the old island style, with an interior courtyard and a fountain. The poet Valaoritou is said to have lived for some years in this house. I do not go there too often and I never stay too long, because I value these visits, and the talks I have with Doctor Hogan. He is kindly and humorous and knows much about the island.

We sat in the courtyard for an hour or two, in the shade of the lemon trees, talking of general things. I asked for news of his children—he has a son at the English School at Bebek, and a married daughter in England.

It was pleasant there in the courtyard with the wisteria, and the dark lemon leaves, and the water playing. Maria, the doctor's wife, brought some sweet red Samos wine and fresh figs—the figs are ripening now, Excellency. Pleasant, yes, but I could not relax, my fears refused to leave me. The doctor's presence, the kindly irony of his glance, the amiable dishevelment he always exhibits, the order and tranquillity of his whole establishment—all this failed to have its usual calming effect.

However, I learned from the doctor the identity of the man Mister Bowles was with today. I described him—the thick body, the gaps in the teeth. "That's Smith," the doctor said at once. "The American. He was here only a few days ago."

"What, here in the house?"

"Yes, he brought one of his crew, an Italian. Fellow had cut his hand very badly."

"That's the man with the caïque, isn't it? The one who is fishing for sponges."

"Yes, that's right."

Here was a piece of news. Had their meeting been planned or accidental? They shook hands at parting. . . .

"He's leaving soon, apparently," the doctor said. "Or so Lydia says. I looked in on her today and we gossiped a bit."

How does Lydia know that, Excellency? Obviously she is in touch with the American. Or did Mister Smith tell Mister Bowles today that he was leaving, when they met in the bar? In that case Mister Bowles could have passed on the information to Lydia when he met her after our talk in the bar.

"When was that?" I said. "When did you see Lydia?"

"Round about noon. Why do you ask?"

"I wondered if Mister Bowles was there. At the studio I mean."

"Bowles? No, he wasn't there."

It must be Lydia, then, who knows the American's movements. Perhaps it was she who introduced him to Mister Bowles. If my theory of the gun-running is correct, and if Lydia knows about it, knows who the contacts are, she may have used this knowledge to put pressure on the American. For Mister Bowles's sake, of course. What story can he have told her? Is he trying to arrange a passage on the American's boat? Is he planning to leave in a hurry, cheat me out of my share. . . ? The thought brought me out in a cold sweat.

"We don't see much of you these days, Basil," Doctor Hogan said.

"I have been spending a lot of time at home lately," I said. "Reading, that kind of thing."

I felt his eyes on me, but he asked me no questions. "The news from Constantinople is very bad, so Lydia tells me," he said. "I don't know how she knows these things. I've had no letters for a month. The postal service seems to have broken down completely."

"Why?" I said. "The news has been bad for years, but things go on much as before. What's wrong now?"

"Just about everything, as far as I can make out. They are proclaiming a republic in the north. The Sultanate, the

Caliphate, the whole structure—it is all toppling over, Basil. Abdul-Hamid never leaves the palace now. He lives behind locked doors with no one to rely on but the women of his harem and his Albanian guard—and how far he can rely on them is doubtful. No, it's all up with him this time. I'm going myself, the day after tomorrow, to bring my boy back here."

I am merely reporting what he said about you, Excellency. I am not saying that I believe it. You have ruled for more than thirty years, and in that time there have been many crises.

All the same, I was depressed. When I stood up to go, I was attacked by a slight fit of dizziness. I did not speak of this to the doctor, but his eyes were on me, and he must have seen something change in my face, for he said, "You must take things easy, Basil. I don't like your color much."

"Oh, I'm all right," I said. I was touched by his concern, but any intention I had had of confiding in him had quite gone by now. He is kind, he is even good, but his life is too different from mine, too settled and secure. I need an outcast to confide in—a powerful outcast. Perhaps that is what you are, Excellency. The atmosphere of peace in the house, the sense of an ordered life, of family affection, reciprocal duties and ties, all the things that I have never had, can never have now, all this puts distance between us.

"By the way," I said, as I was leaving, "does the name Mannfeldt mean anything to you? It's a firm of some kind."

"Mannfeldt? Yes, they are the armaments people. Aircraft too I think, not the engines, the bodywork. They've got all sorts of interests. Very big people. Gesing would know more about them, I should think."

"Yes, I'll ask him," I said. "I heard the name, you know, and I wondered. What about *terra rossa?* It came up in the same conversation."

"*Terra rossa?* Red earth. No, you've got me there. Sounds like a name on some primitive kind of map. You know, like *terra incognita* or *terra periculosa.* One of those maps the old explorers made."

"Yes," I said, "it does sound like that, doesn't it? Oh well, it doesn't matter."

I shook hands with them and thanked them. Maria gave me a jar of homemade tomato paste. She put it into my hand as I was leaving. "Come again when you feel like it," the doctor said. I have the feeling that I will never see them again.

I went down a little away along the earth road that descends from the house toward the town. But this road is winding and offers no shade, so I decided to take a more direct way, down the hillside, through the olive terraces. It was late afternoon now, hot and still. I caught glimpses of dark blue sea through rifts in the olive trees. Smell of marjoram, cistus, and mint from the uncultivated slopes among the terraces. At first my own body was all the movement, all the noise there was. Then, within my own pauses, the interstices of movement, I became aware of the life around me, sudden soft impacted sounds among the dry grass edging the terraces, wings of small birds in the trees. Suddenly I looked down to a clearing, a good way below me, and saw a little group, two men and a boy standing together. The fleece of a sheep lay beside them. The sheep itself I saw last of all. It was skinned and strung up on a post or perhaps suspended from a branch. Forelegs tugged high by the rope, livid pink shape in the broken sunlight among the trees. In the last few moments before my line of vision was obscured, I saw one of the men cut downwards from the join of the animal's forelegs. I did not see the knife, only the long cut down, from forelegs to belly. A thick, dark red line followed the knife. I saw this one gesture in just this one moment, then passed on. It was as if it had been performed just for me. Blood, that darker line? No, the animal was dead, blooded already. Probably the darker inner flesh opening to the knife . . .

Down to the lower terraces, out on to the road again, and it was here that Izzet, accompanied by a big, silent, ragged man, was waiting for me, at the turn of the road, just before the first houses. They were waiting at the side of the road, in the shade of the large mulberry tree there. They stepped out into the road before me, forcing me to a stop. Neither of them said anything at first; this silence, and the fact that they had waited so patiently for me there, frightened me badly. I tried to explain to Izzet, but he did not listen. They were not there to listen. We moved to the edge of the road and they stood close to me.

"We know you have seen him," Izzet said. "You were watched."

"He wants two more days," I said. "In order to complete his researches."

"He said nothing about his researches yesterday. It was he who fixed the time. He was in a great hurry then. Now he wants more time."

"Please have patience," I said. "You know the Englishman is honest."

"Honest?" Izzet smiled, very disagreeably. The ragged man smiled too, I think because he saw Izzet smiling. "He has been seeing the American," Izzet said. "The American has a boat. Do you think we are fools?"

"No," I said. "Of course not. But you should not attach any importance to these meetings with the American. It is natural for foreigners who speak the same language to be on friendly terms."

"Why only now?" Izzet said. "Tell me that. You cannot. Basil *Effendi*, you are in great trouble."

They were standing very near. The ragged man reeked unpleasantly. Their shadows were over me and over the reddish dust of the road: Izzet's quick and small, moving with his gestures; the ragged man's motionless. Beyond them the road was stained and sticky with fallen mulberries and flies were murmuring among them.

I said, "I will speak to him. As for the boat, I am sure there is no connection." I attempted to move further down the road, but they moved to prevent me.

"You know Mahmoud Pasha," Izzet said. "He is not a patient man." There was something more than threat in his voice, something almost confiding. It occurred to me then

136

that Izzet too might be in some fear. He and I are similarly placed—acting for unpredictable principals, seeing our respective dreams fading. "He has no chance," he said. "Tell him that. The soldiers are no longer on the site itself, but the approaches are watched, from above, from below. He has no chance at all."

"I will tell him," I said.

They moved aside at last, and I went on down the road, still clutching my jar of tomato paste. I was shaken by the encounter, Excellency. I feel a kind of half-incredulous horror now, when I recall it. Here in my room, among the accustomed things, it is difficult to believe that anyone, anything, could have such power over me. The table before me, the words on the page, the life they assume: is it possible that the expression on another man's face can prefigure the eclipse of all this? Even while my flesh shrinks with fear of the knife, my mind swells with arrogance. I am the spinner, the creator. I am at the center of my inviolable world . . .

But why do they delay? Why do they deal so delicately with us? It is not the *Vali's* usual method. Are they so afraid of repercussions from the British Consul in Smyrna? Smyrna is far, Constantinople is even farther. By the time an investigation was ordered, they could have plundered the site, without witnesses. Then who is to say what was found and what wasn't? (There is nothing there, of course, but they do not know that.) Perhaps they are hoping to catch Mister Bowles *in flagrante delicto,* so they can proceed with an appearance of legality. No, this too could be easily fabricated. They must have some other reason for their unwillingness to risk an inquiry, something that Mister Bowles himself knows nothing about. My mind returns to that red quadrilateral on the map in Mahmoud's office. Odd that the doctor should mention maps. A primitive kind of map, he suggested, of the sort made by the old explorers. Or navigators, of course. What other people make maps like that? People who want to indicate where treasure is buried. We are back to Mister Bowles again. What possible connection could there be with Mannfeldt? Besides, the phrase was not on the map at all, it was in the letter. Gesing would know, the doctor said. Yes, Gesing must be involved in it somewhere. The frequency of his visits, the deference with which he is treated. They are armament manufacturers. Perhaps Herr Gesing is acting for them, trying to get a contract to supply items of equipment to the Turkish army. But why here? That sort of contract is only to be obtained in Constantinople, through government channels. The letter came from Constantinople, of course . . .

The news from Constantinople worries me the more I think about it. It is not only the doctor who says that your throne is toppling; one hears the same thing on every hand. They say that you keep yourself locked away in your palace at Yildiz, for fear of assassins; that you never emerge, not even for the Friday visit to the mosque; that your troops in Macedonia and the northern provinces are openly in revolt and preparing to march on the capital; that you are without support except for your women and eunuchs and the palace guard—who are themselves owed their pay, and probably disaffected—in short, Excellency, that the whole edifice of your administration is about to collapse. There are even rumors that you are already deposed, already dead.

I must not, will not, believe this, Excellency. I need so desperately the continued splendor of your existence. To whom, other than you, can I address my reports and my prayers, surrounded as I am by enemies, with no word of acknowledgment from your officials? You are my only hope. It makes no difference whether I send this report or not. It is your existence that matters. If you cease to exist now, Excellency, I am extinguished with you.

How well I remember your accession, though I was no more than a boy then. All day the streets were crowded with people waiting. They came from many parts to see you. The rich came in coaches, black eunuchs riding with drawn swords alongside. All day the people squatted in the street, waiting, smoking. When the sun rose and it grew hot the sellers of sherbet and melon did a great trade. My mother bought me *lukumi* wrapped in painted paper. I remember still the blue and red designs, the sweetness dissolving in my mouth, the thirst following. Everyone was happy. Then the soldiers marching through the streets, to take up their positions in the courtyard of the mosque, the Albanians in their plumed hats, the *Spahis* in silver and blue, the *Bostangis* most resplendent of all in scarlet and gold. You came to Eyub on a white horse, the green banner flying over your head, music playing, the people cheering. We could not get very near to the mosque, because of the crowd. But we waited there, as near as we could get. Then the voice of the *imam*, proclaiming your reign. Commander of the Faithful. God's Vice-Regent on earth. What expectations we had of you, Excellency.

I have decided to go up there, tomorrow morning. Up into the hills. I must find out what is happening. I made up my mind this evening in the cafe—I went to the cafe on the square, after my meeting with Izzet. The one that is opposite the hotel. I sat there an hour, watching the entrance, but he did not come. I knew he would not. I sat there, looking sometimes across at the entrance, sometimes down at my inert thighs in their crumpled white, my plump but delicate hands. As if looking for evidence of something—of my existence, perhaps. Nobody joined me at my table, but old Panos the waiter talked to me from time to time, and he smiled. He did not stay near me, but he spoke, on three occasions we exchanged words, and these interchanges made me more aware, not less, of the hush always around me these days. At the center of this hush, there is my mind, noting things, framing words. Flowers on the stall, people passing, Yannis standing morosely in the evening sun at the hotel entrance—I can only make these things exist by naming them, interiorly mouthing the words. But why did Panos speak to me? We were never friends. Has he not heard the stories? Perhaps he is unswayed by them. Could it be that I am mistaken, deluded, that there is no feeling against me? Impossible; have I not seen it on their faces, do I not see it a hundred times a day? When I try to decide whether it is really so, try to recall precise events, expressions, my mind refuses; the hush in which I live takes on a quality of sibilance, a faint hiss; my head aches and I feel nausea. I cannot bear these uncertainties any longer, uncertainties about your existence and my own. I must go up to the site tomorrow.

Revelations, Excellency. I know now why Mister Bowles delays.

It is afternoon, about the third hour. Light outside, but my shutters closed, lamplight on the paper before me. The white sheets and my words on them clear in the soft light. I have a sensation of lightness, almost of floating—I am not heavy enough in my chair. Perhaps due to hunger. I have eaten very little today. Strange this lightness, this insufficiently anchored feeling, because my body should be tired, should be exhausted after the exertions of the day. What could better illustrate the dualism of soul and body?

I left early, at sunrise, dressed as I had been on that earlier occasion when I watched them among the rocks. I am not used to walking, and progress was slow once I had gone up from the shore into the foothills. The sun was high over the sea when I reached the side of the gorge, and fiercely hot on my back as I climbed. This gorge, narrow and very deep, lies at a right angle to the line of the shore. It rises higher on the far side, then tilts down in a long gradual line to form the promontory. The ruins that Mister Bowles is so interested in lie beyond this, on the downward slope. To reach them from here it was necessary to work round the neck of the gorge through tangles of rock and scrub. I had calculated that this route would bring me out more or less directly above the ruins. If I proceeded cautiously I should be able to approach without attracting the attention of anyone already there.

It was intensely hot. The pulsing of the cicadas was almost intolerably loud, drowning all other sounds. Wavering clouds of tortoiseshell butterflies rose around me, disturbed from their feeding on the origan flowers. Already I was feeling exhausted. I was paying the penalty for years of sedentary living. My legs ached, I was perspiring freely.

Thoughts of serpents and scorpions came unbidden to my mind. Once I stumbled and fell, bruising my shin. Nevertheless I persisted. I took off my jacket and slung it over my shoulder. I pushed back the headcloth from my sweating brow. The desire to have my uncertainties removed increased with every step. In fact, so totally was I prey to this ardor that my physical discomforts ceased to trouble me; rather they began to be welcomed as a sort of earnest of success. Suffering, too, is a kind of portent. (Let me take this opportunity of saying that I have always wished to suffer, all my life—though it is only recently that I have fully realized this. That is why Mehmet Bey found such a willing instrument in me: not because I wanted to betray, but because I wanted to suffer. That is why I became a writer of reports, Excellency. Otherwise why would I wrestle with words, go on wrestling, when every bout ends with me thudding to the canvas? Easier to stay down, make the submission sign. I see I have used the same word as Mister Bowles. *Instrument.* An odd word for him to use.)

With undimmed ardor, then, I worked my way round the side of the gorge to the long spur of the headland. Now I was in sight of the sea again, glimpsed its far blue through tangles of broom and holly oak. Below me I could see the beginnings of the ruins, traces of walls here and there, discernible as lines and angles rather than structures, signs of a human intention among the otherwise haphazard accumulations of nature. I paused at this point, and it was fortunate I did so, because in this pause I heard voices, higher up, to my right. Moving very slowly, and keeping well below the line of the spur, I made my way toward this sound, and after no more than a hundred meters I saw them, saw the drab olive of their uniforms, two soldiers sitting on a narrow level backed by rock, in the shade of a low pine tree. One sat against the rock, the other was farther forward, looking out toward the sea. I could not see their faces clearly, but their heads were young-looking, close-cropped—they were not wearing their *kepis.* There is room there, as far as I could judge, for bedding and a fire. A good place for surveillance, because although they cannot overlook the actual site itself, they can watch all approaches to it from above, from the interior. I suspect that Mahmoud Pasha has posted at least two more men below the site, on the shoreward side.

They showed no sign of being aware of my existence. With utmost circumspection, using declivities, thin folds in the hills, rocks, bushes, anything that afforded cover, I made my way down toward the ruins. Farther down, concealment was easier as the vegetation grew more thickly; there were trees among the scrub, wild almonds, gnarled abandoned olives, umbrella pines, even some chestnut trees—all this due to the presence of water here, just below ground.

I paused again here, grateful for the shade. Far below I could see the long irregular swathe of green where vegetation clothed the shallow ravine of the watercourse running down to the shore. Beyond this, and appearing like a continuation of it, the ancient jetty pushed into the sea, the water greening over the massive blocks below the surface. The shapes of marble, untarnished by centuries of immersion, glimmered in this light, at this distance, like limbs of some gigantic marine deity sprawling there. Somewhere below me, though I heard no sound, somewhere amidst this denser foliage, if I was right, was Mister Bowles.

I descended, following the green tracery of the spring, scrambling over rock and scrub, clumsy, fearful—yes, I was beginning to feel afraid, Excellency, as if Mister Bowles might suddenly manifest himself, confront me, rise up from among the rocks. I experienced that ancient fear of the watcher or tracker when he suddenly feels that he himself may be the quarry. Vigilance in pursuer or pursued breeds terror.

Nevertheless I persevered, hearing the sounds of my own exertion, hearing too the faint but all-pervasive sound of running water. The going was easier now, I was following a cracked, uneven pavement, partly grassed over. On one side the circular bases of pillars formed the rough pattern of a colonnade; on the other the ground had slipped and fallen away, there were hummocks of rubble softened by grass and ground ivy. The pavement led to a *tholos*, perhaps marking the inner sanctuary of the temple. Beyond this the ground was again heaped and broken.

I took a path between thickets of arbutus, or what at first seemed a path. In fact it was merely a level cleft between outcrops of rock, and led me into another, but much narrower and steeper ravine.

As I moved slowly forward through this defile, my sense of desolation grew, the constriction in my heart tightened. No longer the ardor of discovery, illumination. Now I felt only doubt of surviving in this fearful undergrowth. Perhaps Mister Bowles was not there at all. Why should I have thought that he was? Why was I there myself, what chimera had lured me? Reason dimmed in me, all purpose left me. I was reduced to my own solitary inexplicable existence, an unwieldy, sweating person, uttering intermittent grunts, his life wasted behind him, his prospects minimal. In search of what? I stopped, stood still, and fear for my existence settled round me, closely, intimately. In full summer, in the middle hours of the day, we should avoid lonely, enclosed places, Excellency. Existence is intensified in us, to the point of dread. There was dread in the beating of my heart, in the shrilling of cicadas, the wavering flight of butterflies, the leaps of grasshoppers sustained beyond expectation. Pan's time, when every creature realizes itself, the weak in fear, the strong in power.

I had some moments of swoon there, Excellency. Then, with an effort, I went on, clambered out of this "well of eternity," literally clambered, as the gully had become impassable. I scrambled up one side, clinging to the roots of cistus and sage, onto a more gradual upward slope facing away from the sea. Before me, on the left, were further ruins, low walls, the ground plan of a house. A fig tree grew against the arch of a doorway. To my right, the slope continued, bare, ocherous, scattered with small rocks. Along the crest of the slope a few straggling thorn bushes. As I stood there looking up, I heard, or thought I heard, through the ubiquitous sound of water, a voice, a human voice, male, in trailing snatches of song. I at once began to climb the rise, setting my feet sideways; caution and the effort of climbing keeping my body low. The singing carried to me again. I lay flat, with my breast against the last few feet of the slope. Very carefully I worked my way upward until by raising my head I was able to see what lay on the other side of the slope. What I saw was so extraordinary that I almost despair of making it credible to your Excellency.

The ground fell steeply into a hollow, roughly circular in shape, tangled with bushes immediately below me, then open for a few yards until the land tilted up again, reddish in color and bare, like the slope I had just climbed. Alone there, full in the sun, was Mister Bowles. He was working, slowly scraping with a shortbladed knife at the face of the farther slope. Except for his hat and a pair of white drawers, he was naked. Naked and dark red in color, gleaming with perspiration. Red too, lusterless dull red, was the earth face he was working at. He was singing to himself in a droning baritone; not words, but odd random notes, such as a man makes when he is busily occupied.

At first, in those first few seconds, it seemed to me that Mister Bowles had taken leave of his senses in this hot secret place, and was attacking the very earth itself, in slow maniacal protest against the human lot. But the motions of his knife were too fostering, too delicate and loving. There was no adversary there. Besides, it seemed to me now that I could discern a shape, a form, lurking in the clay: Mister Bowles was engaged in an act of creation, he was carving a form out of the hillside. Stilling my agitated heart, and clearing my eyes, I made out lines of a human figure, largely embedded still, turned a little from me, the contour of a shoulder, a face, the shadow of a face, curiously obscured and indistinct. Man's or woman's? It dwelt there while Mister Bowles, like some devotee in his hat and drawers, made worshipful motions with his knife and droned his song.

It dwelt there, yes. He was not carving it. Not sculptor but midwife, freeing the form from its impedimenta, its gross obscuring matter, *delivering* it. This is the task that has been absorbing him, this the reason for all his prevarication and delay.

I watched him for some time longer, in fascination. Then I began to think about getting away. It struck me as distinctly unwise to announce myself there and then, even dangerous. I thought it best to steal away and deliberate on how best to use the knowledge thus unexpectedly gained. However, *dis aliter visum*. Along the crest of the slope where I was lying the earth was loose and friable. In shifting my position preparatory to retreat, I dislodged several small stones and one or two larger ones, which slid a few yards down the slope behind me until caught in the scrub. Unfortunately for me, Mister Bowles was not singing just at this moment, and he heard it. He turned at once and very quickly. I ducked down below the crest. There was silence for some moments and I was beginning to breathe again when I heard his voice, in quite distinct and passable Turkish—*ah, le perfide!*—saying, "Come down here at once." I heard sounds which indicated that he had changed position. I thought of flight, but Mister Bowles is fitter and faster. Besides, there was the revolver.

I raised my head and looked down. I was filled with apprehension. He was at the foot of the slope, on my side, just beyond the bushes. He was holding the revolver. "It is I," I said. "Pascali." Grammatical, in spite of my fear, Excellency.

"Come down here," he said again, this time in English.

I did so, with what alacrity you can imagine. He stood there waiting. Naked, glistening red, that instrument of death steady in his hand. When we were face to face, I saw a look in his eyes that I recognized. I had seen it the day before in Izzet's: not fury, not dislike—a steady look of murder.

When he spoke, however, his tone was almost equable. "What the devil are you doing here?" he said. He had a heavy, sweetish smell about him, mingled sweat and oil—he had oiled himself against the sun.

In fear I told him. I had been curious, I said, and being

curious had made my way up here. Curiosity, I said, was a primal instinct in *Homo sapiens*, and I had my fair share of it. Besides, there had been particularly strong cause for curiosity in this case, because I had wanted to see what a man would risk losing so much money for, not only his own share, but mine. And more than money was at risk, perhaps he did not realize that our lives were in danger. I told him of the meeting with Izzet, how they had waited for me. Talking thus volubly, I saw the look of death leave his face.

All the same he had not really listened. "Professional curiosity," he said, when I had rather breathlessly come to a stop. "Once an informer, always an informer, I suppose." There was something of a sneer on his face.

"Indeed yes," I said, in haste to agree. I was beginning to feel a certain elation, now that he looked saner. I knew the existence of something he had wanted to keep secret. That he could have hoped to keep it secret for long was a sign of his less than total grasp of reality, his belief in the shaping force of his own desire. With troops on the ground, Mahmoud and Izzet intent on recovering the lease, and half the town no doubt aware by now of his interest in this place among the hills, it can only be a matter of time before his *trouvaille* is common knowledge. Perhaps even now there are others who know, others who have watched . . .

He went over to where his clothes were lying and bent down. When he returned his hands were empty. He turned to indicate the form in the hillside. "Isn't it marvelous?" he said, and in those blurted syllables there was a kind of confiding enthusiasm. I think he was glad, now that the murderous desire to preserve his secret had passed, to have found someone with whom he could share the experience. "Too early yet, of course, to identify the period," he said, with an attempt at scholarly dispassion. I was reminded of his manner on producing the articles from the Gladstone bag, the way he had lectured us. His pale eyes in the sun-darkened face looked hallucinated almost.

"By God, yes," I said, taking some steps nearer to it. In fact, the figure gave me feelings of dread, Excellency; or rather, it renewed that dread I had felt some time before, trapped in the gully. It was life-size as far as I could tell, reddish clay-colored, the color of the earth that still largely contained it and into which it was half facing. The contours of left shoulder and upper arm were all that had been so far uncovered completely, the features and head being still partially obscured by encrustations of earth; it was this masking accretion that disturbed me as I went closer. With the beauty of the shoulder and arm revealed and evident, and head and face bemonstered still by those gouts of clay, there was a sense of affliction and stillness in the form, as of some creature arrested by the gods, punished with partial metamorphosis, flesh into earth.

"Bronze," Mister Bowles said. "It is bronze, you know, not stone."

"Male or female?"

"Oh, male," he said at once. "Look at that arm."

It was extremely hot in this hollow. My feeling of oppression increased. It was due, I think, not merely to the heat, or the ambivalence of the figure in the hillside, but to what I felt as the intensities of feeling expended and retained in this enclosed place. Secrecy, aspiration, fanaticism—I know not what to call it. It was in the red earth and pale rock and the bushes and the liturgies of the bees among the thyme. It was in Mister Bowles's face. *Savage* was the word that came to my mind. I am sensitive to atmosphere, as I have told you before, Excellency. All good informers are.

I could feel sweat trickling slowly down my left side. "Beautiful," I said, vaguely.

"Isn't he?" he eagerly and instantly agreed.

"I think I must leave now," I said. "I find it very hot down here. A regular suntrap," I added, attempting a laughing tone.

He paused, looking at me as if considering. "Yes," he said. "It does get hot down here. I'll stay a little while longer. The work is just getting to an exciting stage, you know."

"Quite so," I said.

"Then I've got to clean up a bit before I leave. Fortunately there is water here."

"Yes," I said.

Mister Bowles hesitated again, then he said: "I've got a proposition you might be interested in. Will you come over to my room at the hotel for a drink this evening? I'd like to talk to you. I'd like to explain all this."

"Very well," I said.

"About nine? In the meantime, keep this to yourself."

"Of course," I said.

"You'll be the loser if you don't." Mister Bowles nodded significantly and looked intently at me from under the brim of his hat. "You'll lose everything," he said.

It was with these words echoing in my mind that I turned away from him, started scrambling up out of the hollow. They are in my mind now. How long I have been sitting here, writing to your Excellency, I don't know. I lose count of time here at my table. Time, in any case, is running out for me, as it is for Mister Bowles, and you too, Excellency, I think. I will never get the money now, never get off this island. I must write everything down before it is too late. Already I know with sadness that things have been missed and lost, impressions, complexities of meaning, significant facts even, that will never now find their way into this report. Inevitable, I suppose. Now all my waking thoughts are devoted to this work of mine. Even when I am with others I am formulating phrases, looking for the significant detail with which to enlighten your Excellency.

I have forgotten to eat today and now I am hungry, but there is no food here. Mister Bowles mentioned a drink; perhaps food will be included. Nine, he said. I should think it must be six now, perhaps a little later: the sea has assumed its evening softness and depth, the sky is paling. I must rest a little, Excellency.

The sun had set when I awoke. I made coffee—it is here before me now. I rate the coffee bean above the olive among

God's gifts to man. My legs and shoulders ache from the exertions of earlier. I look from my window at the luminous afterglow on the sea. The sky a gauze-rose suffusion. I look along the shore to the darkening hills where I stalked Mister Bowles today. As the sky loses light the trees along the skyline lose distinctness; they soften like charred wood. Minutes after this charring of the trees darkness will fall, abruptly, like some dark stuff with scents in its folds, smells of dust and pine and the faint brackish odor of the nighttime sea.

Again, as on that first evening, the evening of our meeting, I picture Mister Bowles in his room. He will stand at his window, looking out at the nightfall. How, I wonder, did he become what he is? Natural delinquency or some process of disillusionment? Perhaps he discovered his gift by accident, as I discovered mine. Again I feel that we are kindred spirits. Passionate, fraudulent Mister Bowles. *Mon semblable, mon frère.* How will he keep his bearings in this sudden descent of night? Here in the Levant darkness comes too soon for the stranger, comes before he has time to create his nighttime being. Will Mister Bowles be caught unawares before there is time for the stiff upper lip? It is not like the gradual English nightfall, Excellency, that I have read of in their poets but never seen, resignation coming with the waning light, the waverings of gnats, the last songs of birds. There the heart is given time to attune itself, to find some form of pensiveness or melancholy, not unpleasing. In England they are schooled in this gentle stoicism, but how does he feel here, with darkness imposed like a gesture—almost a gesture of extinction? I see him for these few minutes at the window, overtaken by darkness, with the crooked line of his past behind him and the short straight line in front. He stands there, aware of aspirations disappointed, ambitions unfulfilled. And now just one ambition, simple and immense, overriding everything.

Excellency, I now know what *terra rossa* is. And with that knowledge other things have fallen into place. But I must deal first with Mister Bowles.

I went straight to his room. He was there before me, as I expected, but it could not have been much before, because when he opened his door I saw signs of chaos and confusion behind him, saw it even before entering—clothes on the floor, a chest of drawers with gaping apertures where the drawers should have been. He had not had time to put this in order. Where had he been then, while I had been writing, sleeping, writing? He must have left the site well before dark.

"Yes," he said, no doubt seeing my eyes widen. "Someone has been having a jolly good look at my possessions. Come in, anyway. It will not take long to put things to rights."

I sat on the bed, watched him bundle clothes back into drawers, into the wardrobe. "Is anything missing?" I said.

"Not as far as I can see. There's nothing much here except for a few clothes. I always travel light, you know."

"Except for marble heads," I said.

Mister Bowles paused in his tidying, and looked at me. "H'm, yes," he said. "But that was necessary." No slightest sign of a smile on his face. He seems almost totally lacking in humor. Perhaps it is just this deficiency that makes him so successful as a trickster. But it is not enough to explain his unnerving air of being always justified. "They must think I'm an absolute idiot," he said.

"Why?" At this moment, by a fortunate chance, I leaned forward on the bed and as I did so I glanced down and saw the little notebook with shiny black covers lying just underneath.

"To think I would leave anything valuable lying about in my room," he said.

He could not yet have realized it was there. Otherwise, I reasoned, he would immediately have retrieved it. Casually I moved a little along the bed. The diary was now within reach of my foot. "Probably Izzet, or some of his minions," I said. "They will be trying to find out if you have taken anything of value from the site."

"I suppose so," he said. "They stopped me and searched me as I was coming back today. The two soldiers stationed above the site. I don't think they knew what they were looking for. In any case, it is quite absurd. They can't see the site itself, nor a good part of the ground below it. There are a thousand hiding places there."

"It is more serious than you seem to think," I said. "They won't wait much longer. Your *life* is in danger. Mine too."

Mister Bowles was crouching at the chest of drawers with his back to me. I extended my foot, kicked the diary towards me, bent down, picked it up. I had no time to do more than slip it behind my back before Mister Bowles looked round at me. "I'm a British subject," he said.

"You are as liable as any other subject to die of a knife between the ribs," I said. "Take my advice before it is too late," I said. "Let them have the papers back on the terms they have offered."

He straightened and turned to face me. "And the statue?" he said. "You don't understand. I have a responsibility now."

Excellency, I cannot describe the earnestness, the conviction, with which he said these words. I heard in them the final death-knell of all my hopes. It was at this point, I think, that the idea of betraying Mister Bowles began to germinate in my mind, though it is difficult to be precise about beginnings—the seed had no doubt been dormant there a long time, waiting for the right weather, the right blend of fear and disappointment. "But our deal," I said. "The agreement . . . what about that? It is all over, then?"

"Not at all," Mister Bowles said. "All I need is a day or two longer, that's all. That's where you come in, actually. Look, let me tell you how I came to find the statue, then maybe you'll see . . ."

"All right," I said.

"I'm going to have a glass of beer and a sandwich up here in my room," he said. "Would you like to join me?"

In accents I took care not to make too delighted, I assented to this. He rang the bell and Biron appeared almost at once. The sandwiches were ordered, salami for me, cheese for Mister Bowles. While this was going on I managed to transfer the diary from the bed behind me to my side pocket. Biron was polite and attentive, but he did not look at me, he did not look into my face, either then or when he returned with the food and drink.

"I have been wanting to talk to someone about it," Mister Bowles said, as soon as Biron had gone.

Over the beer and the sandwiches, he told me about it, told me in that halting, curiously compelling way of his, with blurts of eloquence and self-revelation. I shall give his own words where they seem particularly vivid or revealing. But for the most part I shall use *oratio obliqua*. In short, Excellency, what follows is Mister Bowles's story transmuted into art. It will help toward the effect, however, if you will try to picture Mister Bowles himself, sitting opposite to me, face dark red from the sun, pale eyes glinting, hair smooth and neat in the lamplight.

He had decided two days ago, he said, to pay one last visit to the site before selling back the lease. To have a last look around, he explained, and complete his notes: "For the book I am writing, you know."

That he should persist with this story of a book surprised me at the time. But then, of course, it is more than a story, much more. I am coming to understand him. I am sure that his interest in the putative abodes of the putative Virgin is quite genuine. His claim to be writing a book, though I feel sure no words of it have yet been written, is no mere falsehood; the book has that degree of existence fantasy can lay claim to, which is considerable—I speak as one who knows, veteran of many solitary triumphs. No he is not a liar; he is an accomplished fantasist, and like all such—like myself, Excellency—both victim and exploiter. All the same, an uneasy doubt remains. Did he really go back there, in the hot afternoon, to write nonexistent notes for a nonexistent book? With Izzet and the Pasha in the net, and payment only a few hours off? Certain it is that something took him back there—if not I should have had my money, should have been in Constantinople now.

Nothing much of the villa was left standing, only a single arch and a broken wall. (It was in a cavity below this arch, if you remember, Excellency, that he claimed to have found the objects he showed to Mahmoud Pasha and Izzet.) However, the ground plan was still there to be seen, and he had begun a methodical examination of the site, noting the details. "I could hear the lizards," he said, "slithering about among the stones while I was working."

Straightening up from his measurements, he had seen, in the face of the rock behind the villa, small rectangular niches, obviously cut by hand, blackened inside, presumably by the flames of devotional lamps. "I have seen the same sort of thing in wayside shrines," he said. Generations of people had come here to light lamps or candles. Prayers and promises uttered in that remote place, from lips long dead. "I noted it," he said. "It was evidence, of a kind. Popular beliefs have to be taken into account, you know." Also, he had thought it the kind of personal detail that goes down well in a book.

Behind the villa the terrain was very irregular, strewn with masonry half-overgrown, mounded with heaps of reddish earth. It was clear, he said, that there had been considerable subsidence of the land here, though not very recently. He had made his way over this, seeking to trace signs of outbuildings, and he had come eventually to the edge of a roughly circular declivity, steep-sided, scattered with rock and scrub. "I don't really know why I went down there," he said. It wasn't as if there were any visible signs of habitation.

"There was nothing there," he said. "It was impulse, pure impulse."

There was in his manner now a new, and disturbing, quality of intensity. It was clear that he was in the grip of his own story. His eyes no longer regarded me closely, but looked at some point midway between us, with a great effort of concentration. It was as if he was in fear of being swamped, rendered incoherent, by the sheer marvelousness of what he was relating.

The cicadas shrilled with what seemed increasing volume all around him, but not, somehow, he said, in the hollow itself, once he began the descent. They seemed to stop on the edge of the slope, so that the afternoon was both loud and silent. He looked around a bit down there, saw nothing of interest, and was about to leave when, again on impulse, pure impulse—he stressed this, Excellency—he walked over and forced a way through the tangle of scrub that grew against the foot of the slope. Nothing there but the same reddish earth and gray limestone—or such at least was his first impression—and he was in the act of turning away, when something glimpsed there, some intimation only half-conscious, registered as it were on the retina of the mind, caused him to look again more closely. Then he saw what he had seen before, but now with full awareness.

It was at first like a curiously curved spur of rock embedded in the hillside, outer edge of some much greater mass. He might have assumed it to be no more than this. He said, "I might have left it, even then," and his eyes were stark at the thought of that appalling possibility. However, something more than accidental about that curving line had come home to him—it was, after all, what had made him look again: the impossibility of the shape's being a merely random formation. "There was something *necessary* about it," he said. He looked at me anxiously, for understanding, for the charity of understanding. "In the last analysis," he said, "there is no resemblance between the forms in nature and the human form, none at all." I mentioned the gnarled shapes olive trees sometimes assume, the way the sea will sculpt human-seeming reclinations in the rocks of the shore. "No, no," he said impatiently. "There is no necessity about any of these things. That is my whole point. That is what I saw. Those other things you mention, rocks and trees and so forth, they are . . . obedient. What I saw in that line was something *urgent*. It is quite different, you see." He was excited at the force of the distinction he was making. He did not want me to discuss it with him, only to understand his feelings, see the wonder.

So he had stepped closer, taking care not to damage the screening bushes—you see, he was already thinking of concealment, Excellency. He looked closely at it, touched it: it was rounded, smooth beneath the flaking clay. It came to him then that this was a human arm.

He shivered, he told me, in spite of the heat in that enclosure. There was something deeply disturbing, unnerving almost, in the discovery that something in the human image might be trapped there. This passed, and a feeling of excitement rose in him. He moved his fingers slowly along the curve. More clay flaked away, allowing him to feel the rounded solidity beneath. There was not enough of the arm exposed yet to establish the dimensions, so he tried removing some of the earth at the sides, but it was packed hard, too hard for his fingers. He climbed out of the enclosure and returned to the area of the ruins, where he found a sharp fragment of marble. Armed with this he returned, and there, in that screened and secret hollow, he set to work, scraping slowly at the earth, carefully prizing it away from the form beneath.

After a while he stood back. He was looking at the shape of a naked human forearm, life-size, fashioned in metal—bronze it could only be. From the angle of this, he judged that the body to which it was atttached was half-turned inward, into the hillside.

"Amazing," Mister Bowles said. "You have no idea how strange it was, seeing it there like that. It was as if it was struggling, itself, to get out."

He had been obliged to leave it at this point, though he

did not say why. He could not stay any longer, he said—there was no time. He had made no attempt to conceal things. In any case, he said, it was not visible, so far at least, from the floor of the hollow. Only someone who did as he had done, forced through the scrub, would have been able to see it. "That's the whole point, you see," he said. "No one would normally . . . I myself . . . I was led to it." So he had left it and clambered up again, out of that charmed place.

He had been surprised, he said, momentarily, when he got out into the open and could see the sea again, to find that everything looked unchanged. "I tell you," he said, "I expected the sea or the hills or something in the landscape to be different, changed, after that. You probably think that's funny. . . ."

"No," I said, "I understand it very well."

"It was such a wonderful experience, you see. The way I was directed to it, you know. I haven't been able to describe it properly. I went back again today—you saw me there. But it is slow work. I am afraid of damaging him."

"So you knew," I said, "that same evening—when you sent the note?"

"Oh, yes. That's why I mentioned the soldiers. They were there, you know, two of them, actually on the site, just a bit higher up from the villa."

"Well, they are still not very far away," I said. "You didn't think they would remove them altogether, did you?"

"There are two more, lower down," he said. "But it doesn't really matter. All I need is a bit more time. And that's where you come in."

"How is that?" I said. I got up, for no particular reason, and walked a few paces across the floor. The movement brought me a view of the sky through Mister Bowles's window, and I saw the full moon hanging there, improbably large, dilated-looking as if resting on liquid.

"If you would go back to them," he said, "ask them for just a day or two more. Until the day after tomorrow. That's all the time I need. That would give me a chance to clean it up, have a good look at it. Have some sketches made, you know."

"Lydia would be able to do that," I said. "Have you told her about the statue?"

"No, not yet. I'd rather you didn't say anything to her about it just yet."

Excellency, I do not believe him. I think Lydia is in love with him, or at least that he has succeeded in making his life and purposes vitally important to her—which amounts to the same thing. I think she has been acting as intermediary for him with Mister Smith. Inconceivable that she should have remained in ignorance about the existence of the statue, when it was taking up so much of his time and attention. Why does he lie to me? Is it because he and Lydia are planning something together?

"So that is your proposition," I said. "I am to go to Mahmoud Pasha and Izzet and ask them to wait until the day after tomorrow. Then presumably you will hand back the lease agreement?"

"Exactly," he said. "And then we shall get our money."

"What makes you think they'll wait?" I said. Actually, I was myself puzzled, as I had been puzzled for some time, by the most uncharacteristic patience being displayed by Mahmoud. The Pasha is afraid of something, Excellency. Something is holding him back—something more than respect for a lease or the rights of a British subject.

"Oh, they'll wait," Mister Bowles said now, with full confidence—it is obvious that he at least believes this. "When we have got our money," he said, "I shall report my discovery to the authorities in Constantinople. The statue will be recovered, it will be taken to Gulhane, where it will be exhibited to the public as one of the new museum's most prized possessions. I will request that a small plaque be placed beside it, giving my name and the circumstances of the finding."

"And that would be enough for you?" I asked.

"It would be there, you see," he said. "My name, I mean. There for all to read."

"What about me?" I said. "Mahmoud Pasha will be furious. He will have no time to explore the site. Officials from the mainland will be here as soon as you report the matter."

"True," he said. "That is quite true, old chap, but you will have the money, won't you? I mean to say, if Mahmoud had paid up and then found nothing, your position would have been just as difficult."

His selfishness was monstrous—the single, absolute nature of his vision. "You should have thought of that," I said, "before you asked me to act as interpreter." It was true that I had intended to leave anyway, once I got the money, make for Constantinople and the archives. But Mister Bowles did not know that. He had been quite prepared to leave me to the wolves.

"Never mind that now," he said. "What do you say? Shall we be allies?" He was smiling. Suddenly he held out his hand. "We two against the whole damn lot of them," he said.

I smiled back at Mister Bowles and took his hand. "Allies," I said. "We will see this thing through together." I was drawing, Excellency, on the vocabulary of adventure-story heroes, dimly remembered. And so, I think, was Mister Bowles.

In that brief interval, between the touch of his hand and the words of response that I uttered, no more than a few seconds, there was born in me the absolute conviction that Mister Bowles is trying to trick me again; and at the same time I felt my own readiness to betray him burgeoning within me.

We toasted our alliance in the remains of the beer. "You will go and see them, then?" he said.

"Yes," I said. "I will."

"There is another thing," he said. "If you really want to help, you can come up to the site tomorrow and lend a hand. There's a lot to do and it is slow work for just one."

"What time?" I said.

"Oh, any time. I'll be there all day."

I left shortly after this. He did not see me down, which

was fortunate, as it turned out, because then I should probably not have stayed talking to Chaudan in the lounge. And in that case I should probably never have found out what *terra rossa* is. It is a type of bauxite, Excellency.

He volunteered the information; I did not ask for it—it did not occur to me to ask. By a happy chance he had met Doctor Hogan earlier this evening and the doctor mentioned it to him. Lucky too was the fact that Chaudan was staying at the hotel that night. He spends most of his time in the north of the island, on what I suspect is a very uncomfortable construction site, supervising the road they are building along the coast. He is glad to escape when he can, and this evening he had managed it. Yes, Excellency, it is bauxite. Nothing to do with old maps, or explorers. Bauxite—and I am quoting Monsieur Chaudan now—is a nonplastic, claylike material. It can take many forms, depending on origin, being sometimes soft and friable, sometimes dense, sometimes porous. It varies widely in color, being found in pink, cream, brown, red, yellow, gray. *Terra rossa* is of a granular, earthy type, and as the name implies, red in color.

But the truly interesting thing, Excellency, is that all bauxites, however they may vary in texture and appearance, contain a very high percentage of *alumina*, the principle ingredient of aluminum alloys. Aluminum: a metal white, sonorous, ductile, malleable, very light, not readily oxidized or tarnished.

I slept well, Excellency—three or four hours of unbroken sleep. Early morning now, just after sunrise. A great calm over everything, first touch of sun on the sleeping face of the sea. I feel this calm in myself, a spent feeling, peaceful, rather desolate. This report is drawing to a close. Things are falling into place. It is always the same: the potential of the beginning, the tremendous scope for action that one's characters have, the excitements of observation and inference that their very freedom allows one; then the gradual, self-limiting process, alternatives scrapped, anomalies eliminated, until we are left with *this* form, *this* sequence, fixed, consistent, *achieved*.

I feel these threads coming together, adhesive, ready to set in their final shape. Mannfeldt, manufacturers of armaments; the diamond shape on the map; Herr Gesing's influence with Mahmoud, his interest in Mister Bowles's activities; *terra rossa*. There are bauxite deposits up there in the hills, Excellency. That is why Mahmoud Pasha has been buying up the land. Not to negotiate directly with the company—the government will handle the concession—but to be in a position to claim compensation. He could hope to recover at least treble his outlay. No doubt there has been some private arrangement between him and Herr Gesing, who will be working on commission. Something they would not wish the authorities in Constantinople to know—perhaps Herr Gesing has been promised a share in the profits from the resale, in exchange for advance information. I suspect that the compensation offer has already been made, already been accepted. Quite possibly the land is no longer Mahmoud's, but yours, Excellency—acquired as a preliminary to negotiating with the mining company. That would account for Mahmoud's otherwise unaccountable delay in acting against Mister Bowles, his fear that the documents would get into the wrong hands. No punishments so savage as those handed out by a corrupt administration defending its own privilege, Excellency. Mahmoud's extortions and murders here would be overlooked, since they only affected a subject people. But irregularities in respect of imperial property would ruin him, if they came to light. He must have known this from the start, but his cupidity got the better of him. He must have supposed, too, that the lease would run out long before any mining operations were begun. . . .

As for Mister Bowles, I have been looking at his notebook again. Those meticulous entries mean more to me now. There, accurately dated, with the place names in red ink, are the records of his transactions. Over the last six months or so he has been performing all over Asia Minor. Imagine it, Excellency. The same air of rectitude, the same impression of stupidity, the same objects, the same Gladstone bag! And now, after so much endured, so much fantasy sustained, so much self-contempt warded off, now life has outstripped his art, reality has transcended the dream. Can you wonder that he has become so passionate, so possessive?

There are still questions, of course. Why did Mister Bowles go back to the site that afternoon, when the deal had already been concluded? What had he been discussing with Mister Smith that day, when I saw them outside the bar, laughing together? Above all, knowing what I know of him, can I believe that he will surrender the statue to the authorities? *The day after tomorrow.* Why was he so definite about the *day?* It is the first time that he has committed himself in this way.

I do not believe him. That flower of betrayal, which grows with its own urgency now, outside my control—I feel its petals expand. It luxuriates in my distrust of him, and its scent is sickening, desolating. A swamp plant, Excellency, growing in the corruption of my hopes, just as fantasies have flowered in his, in Mister Bowles's.

I will go up there again soon, to fix the few threads remaining.

I T IS DONE. I have been to Izzet—but not to ask for more time. I have betrayed Mister Bowles, the flower is in the light of day now. I did not do it for money, though money was the pretext I carefully fashioned for myself. Even that was unnecessary, because there was money here, waiting for me when I returned from seeing Izzet. An envelope under the door, containing exactly my share of the money, one hundred and fifty liras, and a note, written hastily in pencil, unsigned: *Here is the sum we agreed on. I advise you to get clear of the island without delay.*

It cannot be Mister Bowles who delivered this: he is still up there, on the site, cherishing his bronze boy. If not he, then who? Lydia, it could only be Lydia. He would never have confided in anyone else. Not Mister Smith surely; he will be keeping out of the way for the next few hours. Besides, Mister Bowles would not trust him. No, it must be Lydia, she is the only one he could count on, whose money he could count on. That is why he brought her in, not for the sketches as he pretended to me, but for the money—Mister Smith will have to be paid, and his price for such an undertaking would be high; the Englishman could not meet the bill, presumably.

All the same, it was sent at his behest. He honored his promise. He recognized the contribution I had made. There is even, in the note, care for my welfare and safety. And I have betrayed him. Perhaps at the very moment I was putting the knife into his back that envelope was being slipped under my door. The money has not made my act superfluous, because it was not the motive; but it gives me a feeling of love for Mister Bowles. Not gratitude, love. Also it renders the flower more repellent. In a few hours from now he will be in the hands of the authorities, who are also denizens of the swamp. It will be perhaps the last arrest your accredited representatives on this island will make, because your power too is at an end, Excellency. You too, the king alligator, you are finished too.

Excuse me for the bitterness of my tone. Let me try to preserve coherence in my narrative, even at this late stage; due distance, a semblance of order. I will begin with my visit to the site today, my second visit and I fervently hope my last. (But Izzet told me to remain here, await instructions, and I fear they have plans for me still.)

I set off early. I kept well down below where the soldiers were stationed. They were probably still sleeping, but I took no chances. Mister Bowles himself had not been there long when I arrived. He had brought wine and bread and to-matoes, and he shared this food with me; we ate it together sitting against the bankside in the shade—the sun had not yet risen high enough to reach the lower part of the hollow, which still had the cool of night in it.

After we had finished eating we set to work, each armed with a long-bladed knife. Mister Bowles brought these. He had got them, he told me, from a stall in the market. Presumably they are leftovers from the Sacrifice *Bayram*. Mister Bowles worked on the line of the body turned outward, I on the other side, cutting deeper into the hillside, hollowing out the earth behind the head and right shoulder. We had to be careful not to cut too much away behind, especially in the lower part, as there was a danger of disturbing the balance of the figure, which, as I have said, stood up-right.

We worked like this for perhaps two hours. At regular intervals one or other of us would step back and survey him. Little by little the naked body was assuming shape under our hands. There were no longer those disfiguring gouts of clay which had produced dread in me by bemonstering the features. The metal was still clay-colored, and clay was crusted in the ears, the corners of the eyes, the folds of the lips, the short curling hair; but the proportions were clear now, the level brows, the line of the chin, the strong column of the neck.

As we worked Mister Bowles talked to me. His hesitations and plunges seemed less strange here, the rhythm of our work providing a sort of accompaniment. He had always, it seemed, been interested in the ancient world. "Ever since I was so high," he said, holding out his knife. At school it had always been the ancient history lessons that he liked best, looked forward to most. "The very names," he said. "Sumerians, Babylonians . . . And then the idea that you could dig, find out things about them . . . When people asked me what I wanted to be, you know, I always said, Archeologist." But his father had died when he was four-teen, there had been difficulties with money, he had had to go and work in an insurance office, marine insurance, in the city of London. "How I hated it," he said. "Totting up figures all day long, you know. I was there for ten years. Until my mother died." I thought of his little notebook, the neat columns there. It was probably in the insurance office that he had acquired this orderly habit. Was it there too, I wondered, during those ten years' slow rage, that he had seen his mission in life?

I was silent for some minutes, prizing away the earth from behind the neck and below the right shoulder. The face was raised slightly, as if in faintly smiling response to some greeting, or perhaps summons. "What happened then?" I asked him. "Oh," he said. "I gave it up, you know. I mean, there was no longer any reason . . . I started off on my travels. Rather like that doctor, Doctor Hogan. That's why I was so interested. There was a sort of parallel."

I forebore to point out the differences. Mister Bowles too, then, is a believer in portents and parallels. Like myself, Excellency—again there was this slight shock of recognition. The difficulties I have had in seeing Mister Bowles clearly have derived from the fact that he is too close.

By now we were full in the sun. Mister Bowles had stripped to his shorts again, and applied more of that sweetish-smelling oil. I retained shirt and trousers, for fear of being burned by the sun. "I read everything I could," he said. "I kept up with the latest discoveries. When I was a boy, Schliemann was my great hero, you know." He paused, glancing across at me. "Those things I told them," he said, "they were historically accurate. The facts, I mean. I never . . . In all the time I have been traveling around, I never gave false information. Everything I have said could be supported by evidence." It was amazing to listen to him, Excellency. He had claimed to have found a marble head and a gold bracelet where no head or bracelet had been. And here he was, glancing across at me with his hallucinated eyes, talking about false information. There was, after the incredulity, a kind of logic in what he said—so long as you could believe that the first lie was justified, and Mister

Bowles clearly did believe this. "That head and bracelet," he said, as though reading my thoughts, "I am sure now, in the light of this find, that what I said was quite correct. This villa is undoubtedly the site of a considerably earlier house. You only have to look at the foundations to see that. I am convinced that this statue was part of a collection formed during the Attalid period. Perhaps someone from the mainland who had a country house here. That is the only time that would correspond to the date when there would have been anyone in this part of the world rich enough or cultivated enough to form such a collection."

"How do you think it got here?" I said.

"Anybody's guess," he said. "It certainly wasn't made here. Shipped from Greece to Asia Minor, I should say. Then, some time later, here. You can see how the land has subsided very considerably all over this part of the hills. Quite possibly the earlier house was destroyed in that way. Who can say? We're talking about two thousand years. He has been here, in the hillside, for two thousand years."

Upon this, I stood back again to look at him. He was free now to the waist. Below this he was exposed in low relief, still backed against the clay. He was a very young man— shapely and strong, but slender—not quite yet at the full growth of manhood. Though discolored with tarnish and ingrained with clay, nothing of him that we could see was broken or incomplete. The features, fingers, genitals, all were perfect. One arm, the one turned to us, was held somewhat away from the side, bent at the elbow, the forearm extended forward of the body at an angle slightly below the horizontal. The hand was open, fingers spaced a little. The other arm was at his side. He appeared to be taking a short step forward, the right leg being a matter of nine or ten inches in advance of the left, though both feet rested flat on the same level, thus throwing the weight of the body slightly back, contradicting the apparent intention of forward motion. This tension in the form gave an appearance of hesitation to the pose, reinforced by the blind face, the smiling curve of the caked lips.

"He's marvelous, isn't he?" Mister Bowles said. There was a shy ardor in his tone. He might have been showing me a photograph of some loved person.

"He is, yes," I said, and my assent was unforced, Excellency. It was now very hot in the hollow. "I think I'll go and find a bit of shade," I said. "Rest for a while, if you don't mind."

Mister Bowles pursed his lips, as if dubious. Then he said, indifferently, "All right, if you like." He did not really want me wandering around. "Time is short, you know," he said. "I was hoping you could help me clean him up a bit later on."

"Of course," I said. His reluctance was encouraging, in a way. I had other reasons—other than tiredness, I mean—for wanting to break off for a while. I wanted to have another look at the terrain. A certain idea had been burgeoning in my mind all morning. Of course, I had been suspicious of him ever since I had seen him with Mister Smith that day, in the bar—is it two days ago or three? I lose count of time, Excellency. I had thought it possible he might want to buy a passage off the island on Mister Smith's caïque. Perhaps he wanted to forestall the consequences of Mahmoud's fury when it was found that the site contained nothing valuable. Perhaps he was arranging to decamp in a hurry, so as to cheat me of my share of the money. However, finding him with the statue had made me think again. It had explained why he delayed, why he jeopardized everything: he was the prey of his obsession, I had thought, this terrible truth he had found through lies. In all this I had forgotten the more calculating aspects of Mister Bowles's nature, forgotten, too, his sense of being specially appointed. He has been "led to" the statue, as he believes. Does he really intend to give it up for the sake of his name on a plaque? Now I remembered—what I should not have forgotten—that it is not a question only of Mister Bowles and Mister Smith. There are three others on that boat—five men altogether. Five men can do much, Excellency, if paid enough or frightened enough.

I climbed out of the hollow on the same side as I had first approached it, the side from which I had approached it today. From this side it would clearly be out of the question. I knew that in advance. The mounded, hummocky ground beyond, with its tangles of masonry and vegetation, its ruined walls, its steep clefts and gullies—clearly impossible from this side. The statue must weigh three hundred and fifty pounds at least, I had calculated. Quite possibly more. But from the other side of the hollow, the side I had not seen? . . .

I went back toward the ruins until I reckoned I was at a safe distance from him, then began to make my way round in a fairly wide semicircle, with the intention of coming out at a roughly similar level at the other side. This I found extremely difficult, at times even hazardous—particularly for one so unathletic as myself, Excellency. But I persevered. Sometimes on hands and knees, sometimes slithering feet first, torn by scrub and bruised by stone, I made my way round. I was uneasily conscious that parts of my route might have been visible from above, from where the two soldiers were stationed, but though I may have been seen I was not challenged. When I did reach the other side of the hollow, what I saw soothed my pains to a large extent. It was possible, Excellency. For a group of determined men it was feasible, though difficult. There would be five of them, if all the crew were employed on it. Excellency, supposing I am right about Mister Smith. Supposing he is here on some illegal enterprise—let us say landing guns for the rebels. And supposing something has gone wrong. Perhaps being searched has scared him. Perhaps there has been some breakdown in the arrangements. In this situation he will be wanting to get away, he will be interested in the idea of some quick money. Not threats, as I once thought—men like that would be too dangerous to threaten. But money, yes. And Lydia has money. . . .

I had come round from the side, through rock and thick scrub into a more open area, not precisely behind the hollow where Mister Bowles was working, but giving me a view of the slope down from this, and then the longer, more gradual slope of the hillside itself. It was true that there were sizable rocks amid the pine trees, especially on the first and steeper part of the slope, and there were folds in the ground that might be awkward. But no more than a hundred yards beyond, quite clearly visible, was the line of the stream bed—dry now and wide enough for two men abreast. Admittedly, the footing would be difficult, because of the irregular stones forming the bed, but these would not be large, and the slope was fairly gradual. I could not see its course for very far, but I remembered, as I crouched there, the view I had had from the path higher up, on my way here that first day when I had come to spy on him: the long green swathe of the stream bed with its edging vegetation, the sea, the continuing line of the jetty, the greening of the water over the marble blocks. It was possible, Excellency, it was the only possibility, and therefore it must be the answer. They could never get him out of the hollow unaided, of course—a dozen men could not have done it; the slope was too steep, the clay too crumbling. But with lifting gear from the caïque . . . They might have a spare block and tackle. Or they could use the tackle from the boom. It was level enough along the top for three men at least to stand together . . .

There were the soldiers, of course, to reckon with. The two above would see nothing of it; their view was cut off by the fall of the land. But the two below, nearer the shore, they were on the same side of the headland as the stream bed. Besides, there was the noise . . . Mister Bowles had not seemed particularly worried about the presence of the soldiers, once they had been removed from the site itself.

I judged I had been away no more than half an hour. But I do not think, after that scramble, that I could have looked like a man who had been resting in the shade, and I thought that his manner was suspicious when he greeted me on my return. I say that I thought so, Excellency—it was impossible now with him to be certain of such things.

His wild and gleaming appearance made normal identifications impossible. His whole manner, since the finding of the statue and the subsequent secretive labors, had become so charged with feeling, so almost *melodramatic*, that there was no register for milder feelings.

"I don't think we'd better dig round him any more," Mister Bowles said. "I don't want him to start keeling over. What I'd like to do now is clean him up a bit. I've been bringing olive oil up here. That was the only thing I could think of that wouldn't damage the surface, you know."

He had also brought several cloths, squares of black velvet—thick, heavy velvet such as is not to be had on this island, Excellency. They had been cut roughly from some single piece, perhaps curtaining or a woman's dress. I wondered where, at such short notice (since he could not have known he would need it), he had been able to obtain such material.

We worked together, Mister Bowles on the head and face, I lower down on the pectoral slopes and rib cage, applying the oil gently but firmly, softening by repeated application the encrustations of clay. From time to time I glanced up at their two faces, the faint impervious smile of the metal, the almost painful care and devotion of the flesh—he was worshipping, Excellency. In me too, as I worked on, there grew up a feeling of reverence. We were *bathing* him, not washing. There was a lustral, expiatory quality in what we were doing. Mister Bowles and I were at one, for the first and only time, ministering together; all I had felt about our closeness, our identity, was evidenced and made tangible here by our hands as we went through the same cherishing motions, repeatedly applied the oil, wiped away the dissolving clay, informer and trickster, divided by our schemes but at one in this ritual.

The clay was tenacious. It clung to him, to the nostrils, the short curling hair, the slight ridges of muscle at the loins, as if reluctant to give up its claim. First applications turned it a glistening darker red, a dark blood color, so that at first we seemed to be washing the body free from the blood of wounds. But below this the metal came up lustrous.

"If I were you," Mister Bowles said suddenly, "I'd get clear of this island as soon as I possibly could. As soon as you get the money, I mean." He did not look at me as he said this, being intent on the eye sockets. There were no eyes, Excellency—below the lids narrow vacancies.

"Yes," I said, "I was intending to go to Constantinople."

"Why there?" he said. "That's the last place I would want to go just now. You won't be able to stay here, you know. There's nothing for you to do here. Not unless you change your profession, or arrange for a new paymaster."

"Why do you say that?"

"The heyday of spies is over," he said, "Abdul-Hamid is finished. The Macedonian regiments are in the capital. They are welcomed everywhere. Enver Bey and Talat are in charge now."

I looked up from my work, at his serious face—he had spoken without mockery—and then up at the blinding purity of the sky. The shrilling of cicadas from the slopes all around us seemed at this moment to rise to a crescendo that was then impossibly sustained.

"Rumors," I said. Even at this moment of shock, my mind continued to assemble evidence against him. It must have been from Lydia that he had got this. He had seen her then, and recently. The velvet material, I was suddenly convinced, had been hers. Quite unexpected and unbidden there came into my mind a recollection from the evening of his arrival, when I had introduced him to Lydia, and seen her hand engulfed in his . . .

"More than a rumor, old boy," Mister Bowles said, stepping back from the statue a little. "It is absolute fact. Why do you want to go to Constantinople anyway? I say, come and stand over here, and have a look at him now."

I did as he said. Although I was still shaken by this curt announcement of your downfall, the appearance of the statue drove everything else from my mind. He stood there, a young man of possibly twenty or so, taking a slight step toward something. His head, chest and arms gleamed in the sun, dark olive color, with glints of gold. The tarnish of ages still lay on the bronze, but the oil had glossed and darkened it. There was no visible flaw in any of the surface we had cleaned. The gleaming torso contrasted with the dull earth color below, giving him the look of someone struggling out into sunlight—an accidental effect, but deeply impressive. Above all it was the tension within the movement of the body itself, something unresolved, disturbingly ambivalent, that gave the work its life and distinction. The form expressed a subtle conflict between advance and recoil. It was there in the raised, slightly smiling face, in the squared shoulders, the tentative gesture of the arm; in the slight forward step and the withheld trunk, which could now be seen to be slightly turned from the direction of the walk, a further torsion of reluctance. With some marvelous instinct the remote creator of this youth had found a form for awkwardness and grace together.

"That is no copy," Mister Bowles said. He turned to me an excited face. "He was already old when the Romans were here," he said.

"I don't know," I said. "He is certainly very beautiful." I was moved, Excellency. Not only by the statue itself but by the way in which Mister Bowles included me in his emotion. Perhaps because of this, perhaps because I intended to inform on him, a great urge to confide in him rose up in me. "You asked me why I wanted to go to Constantinople," I said. "I'll tell you."

And I did tell him, told him everything, as we resumed the work—lower down now, along the flanks and the groin. Told him of the long silence in which I had lived, the neglect of your officials, and now the hostility of the Greeks. "I kept no copies, you see," I said. I told him how the money had come through every month, never varying; and of my wish to visit the archives, bribe my way to repossession of the papers. He listened seriously, though without looking at me. His hat was pulled low against the glare.

"You mean to say nothing has ever happened?" he said. "Good God. As for the money, I have heard of other cases. You know how inefficient the bureaucracy is. They would just go on paying you."

"But twenty years," I said.

"They've been going downhill for ten times as long as that, Pascali. No, there is no machinery for countermanding anything. Some clerk made an order on the bank, and the money keeps on coming. Nobody knows why, so nobody stops it. The chap who arranged it is probably dead. It's not likely he kept any records anyway. Or if he did they would be in such a state of confusion that no one . . ."

He paused, his saturated velvet on the slope of a thigh, and looked across at me. "Just imagine the paperwork involved," he said. His pale eyes looked seriously and directly into mine. I thought I detected in them a look of pity. "Just imagine the weight of it," he said. "The whole system is clogged with paper. Have you any idea how many informers there must be in the Ottoman possessions? The Sultan has been paranoid for years, you know. It is common knowledge that there are more spies than police in Constantinople. Do you really suppose those fellows in the Ministry have a filing system? No one reads *anything*, Pascali."

Because I was frightened by the implication of his words, I took refuge in sneering. "Your own *métier* is at an end, if all you say is true," I said. "Have you considered that? I mean, you depended on this system didn't you? The swamp has been your habitat."

"Swamp?" he said.

"Yes." I was thinking of the flower that was now spreading its petals against the roof of my poor demoralized brain. "The Empire is a swamp," I said, "and if you don't mind my saying so, we both belong in it, together with the orchids and snakes."

"I don't know about that," he said. I think he was embarrassed by my metaphorical language. Rather overdoing things, he probably thought. He himself never used figures of speech. "In any case, I shall be moving on, you see." He raised his eyes to the statue's face. "This is a turning point in my life," he said. "Do you realize how *few* original Greek bronzes there are in existence?"

"I thought you were intending to turn it over to the authorities."

"Oh, yes," he said. "I am, of course. But just the association of the discovery with my name will be enough."

He was lying to me, Excellency. I knew it then, beyond doubt. Knew it in bitterness and desolation. He would never give the statue up. Had he not been "directed" to it? He would go on, as I had always dreaded, follow his dream, while I would be left behind in this place, penniless, among enemies, without an occupation even. I could not endure it. I knew then, finally, what I must do. My eyes were close to the boy's flank. They filled with tears, through which the bronze glinted, became iridescent.

"It is surprising," Mister Bowles said, in a different, more measured voice, "well, at least it always surprises me, how Greek sculpture provides us with a sort of universal paradigm, a model for all human affairs."

I looked up at him from my crouching position. He was standing with his back against the hillside, head turned to look upward along the slope. My eyes were still slightly blurred, and as I looked up at his face in profile, his features had a strange outer edge of light, as if the area immediately adjoining his face derived a radiance emitted from the surface.

"How do you mean?" I said.

"Well, in the very early period, the seventh and sixth centuries, the figures were not really individualized at all. It didn't matter who they were. They were images of man as such. They were marvelously human, but they were not distinguished one from another. Just a celebration of collective humanity, you know. Then you got the breakdown of that sort of mythical unity in the classical period, when there was an awakening to personality, to individual responsibility. It was still monumental—to begin with, at least. I mean there was harmony and balance in it. The weight was in the center. But the unity was achieved in the individual work, not so much in the expression of a collective attitude. As in the sculptures of Phidias, for instance. Perfect unity of form and spirit. But it didn't last long you know. Just that perfect balance, for a generation only, not much more anyway. While it was actually happening, the conditions that made it possible were being undermined. In the Greek state itself things were beginning to break up. There was a lot of conflict—between the individual and the state, secular and religious claims, and so on, and as you come down into the fourth century this shows itself in the sculptures. The center of gravity is displaced from the middle. The figures are not so secure, not so self-contained. There is more differentiation, more insistence on naturalistic detail. Then in the Hellenistic period, you know, after about three hundred, the whole process degenerates into drama and decoration. Instead of that clear arrangement of axes, you get tricks of opposing rhythms. The forms no longer reach out, they turn around their own center. That is the finish of it. The whole art becomes decadent, and so does the society, of course."

"Well," I said, "of those periods you mention, I should have been most at home in the last one, the tricks of opposing rhythms, as you put it—and so would you, I think." In fact, Excellency, although he had spoken in his lecturing voice, there had been a touch of the old moral disapproval in the way he had ended, and it had riled me slightly—hence the gibe, which I do not think he noticed. "I don't see why decadence should be such a dreadful thing," I added.

"Well, the whole thing was fragmented," he said. "You only have to look at the fluctuations of style. You only have to look at the faces, there is no serenity in them. They are questing and doubtful."

"What about *his* face?" I said.

"Oh, him." Mister Bowles's voice softened. My eyes were clear now, Excellency, but Mister Bowles's face still had that radiance about it. He was happy. "He is just at the point of decline," he said. "At the brink. That is why he is so marvelous."

"Fragmented," I said. "That was the word you used, wasn't it? And this whole process took about five hundred years."

"About that, yes."

(That is roughly the duration of your Empire, Excellency. I point this out to you for the sake of the parallel.)

"So," I said, "it went from a collective idea of man, to a very brief period of perfect balance, then to increasing anguish and disunity, finally to breakdown and fragmentaion."

"Yes," he said. "That's about it. We've been living among the fragments ever since."

"Fragments mean pickings," I could not help saying, again provoked by his somewhat schoolmasterly air. "If it could be speeded up," I added, "it would look like an explosion, wouldn't it?"

"How do you mean?"

I looked at him for a moment or two before replying. How strange it was, Excellency. Here we were together, he and I, talking easily; more than that, intimately—we had become friends at last, we had achieved our own, poignantly brief, balance. And I was about to betray him. I felt myself in danger of tears again. "Well," I said, looking away from him, "think of a bomb—a perfect, unified shape, then fragments."

"Yes," he said, "in a way, perhaps, but not really. The true perfection was the balance itself, and that is always an immediate stage, you know. And brief, as I say."

I nodded. "Well," I said, "I can't do much more here. I'll be getting back now, if you don't mind."

"All right," he said. He stood silent while I retrieved my jacket and put it on. "I'll stay on a bit longer," he said. "By tomorrow I shall have all the information I need, you know. Then we can go ahead."

"Yes," I said. "Goodbye then, for the moment."

Mister Bowles hesitated, then suddenly held out his hand. "Thanks for your help," he said. "I won't forget it. Listen, take my advice and don't go to Constantinople. Get out of it all, while the going's good. With your languages you could get work in Europe, as an interpreter, something of that kind."

"It depends on money," I said.

"You'll get your money," he called after me. "You have my word for that."

At the foot of the slope I turned to look back at him. "Tell me," I said, "what did you mean that day, when you said you were an instrument?"

"Oh, that," he said. "Well, someone has to show them."

"Show them?"

"The error of their ways, you know."

"A sort of mission?"

"You could put it like that."

"I see," I said. "Yes, I see."

And I did see, Excellency. I saw several things as I clambered up out of the hollow. Mister Bowles must have had messianic leanings for a long time—perhaps even in those early days, in the insurance office. Now he has come to believe himself sent by a higher power. The delicate balance between zeal and financial gain which has preserved him hitherto, kept him apparently sane among the world of men, an accomplished trickster, has been broken. Whatever *daimon* led him down there in the first place was conducting him straight to mania, to the excess in his own nature which was always there. He went mad in that hollow, Excellency.

At the top of the slope, I turned to look again. He was kneeling before the statue, at work on the belly and loins. I watched the two naked figures together there, the darker and paler red, both gleaming with oil. The youth looked over Mister Bowles's head with a sort of ecstatic aloofness, beyond, to where his step was taking him. That outthrust hand had never held anything, no implement or insignia. It expressed *desire*. The step was made, irrevocable. The body was offered and withheld. Ecstasy may accompany many forms of beastliness and violence, Excellency, as well as communion with the gods; and whether that step forward was into life and joy, or into some degrading rite, could not have been told from the face or posture of the body.

You see I continue to draw parallels, make analogies, even now as the night advances and the moon rises over the sea. Full moon, Excellency—he must have taken this as a sign of favor, of blessing on his enterprise . . . The money is in the envelope, on the table before me, proving that he did not intend to cheat me after all. But I feel no compunction now, no regret, only a sick impatience for the night to be finished. I will break off for a little, with your permission, Excellency, make coffee, rest my eyes.

I left them together, as I have said, Mister Bowles and his bronze love. I knew quite coldly and certainly what I must do. There was no inclination to tears now, only the feeling of desolation which attends acts of destruction felt to be necessary but not really desired.

I felt neither fatigue nor hunger as I made my way back to the town. Occasionally, however, I found myself staggering a little. I went straight to the Metropole, straight to Herr Gesing's room. Just as I was, stained with sweat and clay. If I passed anyone on the way I did not notice. He kept me waiting for some time and when he came to the door he was in crumpled pajamas, puffy-eyed. I had disturbed his afternoon sleep.

"So," he said. "It is you, Pascali."

"Can I see you for a few minutes?" I said.

He looked at me for a moment or two longer, then stood aside for me to enter. His room was bigger than Mister Bowles's. The bed was in an alcove with an arched entrance.

"Here," he said, "take a seat. You are not looking so good this afternoon, Pascali. You like a cold coffee?"

Gratefully I assented. While he busied himself I looked round the room. There were typewritten sheets on the table, but I lacked the energy to try to get a closer look. I

needed no confirmation now. Whether Herr Gesing was acting for Mannfeldt or, as I suspected, some subsidiary interest, possibly a mining company, was of no real interest now.

"I keep always cold coffee, for the afternoons," Herr Gesing said. "In this *verflucht* hot weather."

We sat opposite each other, at the table. Herr Gesing removed the papers, but without haste. "Well," he said.
"What can I do for you?"

Two minutes it took, no more, to commit myself to the
betrayal of Mister Bowles. I did not give any information
to Herr Gesing, and he did not ask for any. I did not by
word or sign indicate that I knew of the bauxite deposits. I
merely made him the offer.

"You said you wanted the Englishman off the land." I
said.

Herr Gesing offered me cigarettes from a japanned box.
"Yes, that is so," he said. "And that is the same now. Our
attitude the same remains."

"Well," I said, "I can get him off. For good. Within forty-
eight hours. But I must be paid."

I asked him for money, Excellency, in a forlorn attempt
to preserve an appearance of reasonable motive, to conceal
from Herr Gesing and from myself the gratuitous nature of
my act. Mister Bowles is intending to be off the island
anyway by tomorrow, if I am right, but Herr Gesing does not
know this. I do not think he knows anything about the supposed finds on the site, nor the deal between Mister Bowles
and Mahmoud Pasha. He may know of the existence of the
statue, but that would be of no great concern to him, probably. Mister Bowles is simply an intruder to him, a potential
threat to his interests.

He smoked reflectively for a minute or two, while I waited,
my head swimming slightly, my vision not clear. "My
name," he said, "must not be . . ."

"Involved?"

"Involved, *ja*. There are interests here, big interests. You
must conduct with care. *Es ist eine lokale Sache*, Pascali. You
understand?"

"Yes," I said.

"Fifty liras. I can give you fifty liras."

"When?" I said. "Now?"

He laughed a little. "No, not now," he said. "When it is done. You come to me when it is done."

"Very well," I said. It did not matter to me, Excellency. The money, I mean. Except, as I have said, to provide a motive. All the same, I thought it probable that he would pay. "Fifty liras is not much," I said, out of a long habit of bargaining.

"Bah!" he said. "Listen to me, the Englishman has no right there, the lease is not in order. In the courts it cannot stand up."

"Yet they allow him to remain there," I said.

"That is what I do not understand." He shrugged his thick shoulders. "But who can understand these people?" he said.

I struggled to my feet. "Don't worry," I said, "the site will be free by this time tomorrow."

"Good, good," Herr Gesing said. His pale fleshy face creased suddenly, revealing a shallow dimple in the left cheek. He held out his hand. "Now we are allies," he said. "Allies, Pascali."

"Yes," I said. I shook his hand. "Commerce and National State advancing hand in hand," I said.

He chuckled. "You remember, eh?" he said. "The future is with us. *Wir haben die Wille.*"

I pictured us as Mister Punch might have depicted us: me as feminine Commerce in helmet and clinging gown, Herr Gesing as National State in a top hat, sausages cascading from below his frock coat. Like the strings of pink sheep guts the Turks carried away after the Sacrifice, for their evening *chorba.* Suddenly it seemed to me that I could smell it again, here in this close room, the stink of blood and sheep pelt that had hung over the whole island. I felt faint; my vision blurred. Then the world cleared again, and Herr Gesing was smiling the same smile.

"A noble ideal," I said.

179

"Not ideal, no. Ideals is nostalgia. Like your Mister Bowles, he has ideals. Bah!" Herr Gesing tightened his small mouth in disgust. "No, ideals we do not have—*wir haben Ziele*, Pascali. *Ziele*."

"Goals," I said.

"Goals, *ja*. The Baghdad Railway, which we Germans have built, that was not an ideal."

"No," I said, moving toward the door. "I suppose not."

I said goodbye to him quickly. Too much to expect that I would linger there with him, talking about Darwinism as applied to national states. Darwin never meant it to be. Besides, I preferred Mister Bowles's perverted idealism to this dirty future of Herr Gesing's, built on one crooked deal after another.

From there I went to Izzet. It did not take long to explain things to him. I did not, of course, tell the whole story. He would have thought me mad. They knew about the statue already—Mister Bowles had been watched. But Izzet was not worried about that. It had not occurred to him that the Englishman would be mad enough to try and remove it; and while he was engaged thus they had felt more secure, since he was neglecting the smaller, more obviously valuable things on the site.

This security I proceeded to destroy. It was not a question of the statue, I said, but of other things.

"Other things?" he said.

"Other things he has found there. Don't you see, Izzet, the statue is only a trick. He has used it to cover up his other activities."

"Why are you telling me this?"

"When I discovered the truth, the kind of man he really is I had no choice. My loyalty to the *Vali* . . . And then, think of my position; I had helped him, you see. You would not have believed me . . ."

"Yes," he said. "Yes, I see." He was already trembling, Excellency. Izzet, as I have said, is very emotional about money. He was far too disturbed to examine my motives thoroughly. "The pig," he said. "What treachery."

"Yes," I said. "He will have a full moon, tonight. They will use the American's boat. They are all in it together."

Touch by touch I inflamed his rage and greed. "I will report this at once to the *Vali*," he said. "You will return to your house, and remain there. You will not leave your house, Pascali."

I obeyed him, Excellency, to the letter. Here I am. It must be somewhere between eleven and midnight. I have heard nothing. Supposing after all that I am wrong. I review the evidence in my mind: the involvement with Lydia; his meeting with Mister Smith; his talk of the day after tomorrow; full moon—he would not dare show lights; the finality of that handshake, and then the envelope under the door. No, I cannot be mistaken. Above all, there is my knowledge of him. He would never give the statue up . . .

Excellency, I hear sounds now, on the terrace outside, voices. They have come for me. What I have been dreading so much I could not speak of it . . . They will ask me to guide them . . . They are knocking now, calling my name.

Everything is finished, Excellency. I am outside the frame now. He is dead. Lydia too is dead. It is more than a week since I have been able to write. I go on living here in my house. No one has made a move against me; I am left alone. It is only with the greatest effort that I take up my pen again. All desire to write has left me, all that racing to keep abreast of things, that passion for recording that has kept me writing so furiously ever since he arrived: all ended now, all stilled. The shots that killed them ended my report. What is left is epilogue, or perhaps, roughly speaking, coda.

They would not have died at all, or at least they would

have been given a chance of life, if it had not been for the discovery of the murdered soldiers. I never intended his death, only his defeat, I wanted to make my failure his too, preserve the intimate connection between us. *Zusammen verbunden*, as Herr Gesing said, that evening at dinner, linking his hands together. All the time, obscurely, I was worried about those soldiers. He did not seem to mind their presence there, once they were off the site itself, away from a direct view of his activities. Did he know what was going to happen to them?

They came for me, Mahmoud Pasha himself and Izzet at his heels. Appropriate of course that I should lead them to him, perform the kiss. Twelve troops. We went in two boats across the bay, keeping near to the shore to be in the moon's shadow as far as possible. They had muffled the oars. We made no noise as we crawled along the rim of the bright sea, the shadowed hills to our right. No one spoke. We beached beyond the headland in the little cove. Their ship's boat was already there, on rollers, near the water. The caïque lay farther out, beyond the line of the jetty, no lights showing. If any of the crew had been left on board, they would certainly have seen us, but there was no sound, no challenge. The boat waiting there on the beach, the deserted caïque, this was all the evidence that was needed. I had been right. They were up there already.

On the beach the soldiers tied cloth round their boots. I too was made to muffle my steps. I had decided to lead them by way of the stream bed, since this was the only way Mister Bowles could come down, and we would thus be able to intercept him if he finished the work earlier than expected.

We proceeded in double file, with myself and Mahmoud in the lead. Mahmoud wheezed with the exertion of the climb, but displayed a dreadful lightness of foot—I was hard put to keep up with him. The smooth stones of the stream bed led up before us white in the moonlight, glinting with mica. We made no noise, trudging steadily, eyes on the path before us, careful of the loose stones. In spite of my anguish, or perhaps because of it, because my mind clamored for respite, a sense of unreality descended on me. I fell into a dreamlike state as we went on, a condition almost of trance. There was the white defile before us, the slow climb, the need to set one foot after the other: all this precluded any sense of an issue, as if this ascent could have gone on forever.

When we reached a level roughly similar to that at which the two lower troops had been stationed, Mahmoud dispatched a man to alert them. They were some three hundred meters to the west of us, in the direction of the town, where they could overlook the approach by sea.

"It is odd," Izzet whispered to me, "that they have seen nothing." His face was pinched and white in the moonlight, looking narrower, more birdlike than ever below the dark turban he was wearing. "The pigs must have been drinking," he whispered.

We waited for perhaps ten minutes there. Then we saw the man returning, walking carefully across the slope, just above us. He was holding both hands extended before him a little, in what even at that distance seemed a stiff and unnatural manner. This was the beginning of the nightmare, Excellency, up till then merely the approaches, the moonlight reaches of the dream. As in nightmare the man was hampered; he could only approach slowly for fear of noise —he had to contain his news until he could whisper it. Slowly he clambered down toward us. He held his hands toward Mahmoud. His broad Mongolian face was expressionless with shock. His hands were darker than his face, much darker—the blood was still moist. "They are dead," he said, in a harsh whisper. He raised one hand and made a sharp gesture inward, toward his chest. "I thought at first they were sleeping," he said.

Mahmoud Pasha looked at the man's hands, then up toward the slope, toward the way we were going. He nodded once. "*Gelde, cochuklar,*" he said. "Come, my children, let us continue."

There was death in the air now—I think from that mo-

183

ment Mister Bowles's death was inevitable. We went on in silence. From time to time we had to climb up along the sides, holding to the low branches of pines. But always we followed the line of the stream. We were now not far below the ruins, though these were not visible to us here. The cold radiance of the moon lay on the hills around and above us. The plunges of granite in the gorge beyond the headland were like streams immobilized by a thickening solution of alkali, divided into deltas by the darker scrub. Threading the slopes, the silver lines of goat tracks.

I led them up, sick at heart, thinking of nothing now but coming to the end. We quitted the track at a point well above the hollow, and very slowly, very cautiously now, came obliquely downward across the slope. He had posted no lookout, Excellency. He would have had the confidence of his destiny upon him, but he must have known the soldiers were dead; otherwise he would surely have taken this precaution—we would have been visible as we took up our positions above them, there would have been time for them to get clear. Of course, he needed all the men for the work, perhaps even Lydia too. . . .

Now the long claw of the headland was before us, beyond it we could see the great brimming expanse of the bay, the glimmering of the ancient jetty, the shadowed caïque at rest on the calm surface. We worked our way around to a rocky terrace on the slope, some three or four yards deep. To our right the land plunged down again in a torrent of silvered rock and scrub. Slowly we worked along the terrace. Suddenly Mahmoud held up his hand, halted us. There they were, Excellency, working full in the moonlight. There were six of them, not five as I had been expecting: two below, in the hollow itself, four at the top of the slope. The statue dangled, still upright, just clear of the bank.

Mahmoud gestured us into position along the terrace, spaced at intervals, concealed among the rocks. Me he kept beside him. It was a perfect field of fire, Excellency: they had no chance, none whatever. And still they worked on, absorbed, totally heedless. Even when his men were settled in position, Mahmoud gave no order. He uttered a hiss of indrawn breath, and when I glanced at him, I saw that he was smiling. I will not forget that smile of his white moon-face. He waited there, withholding the order, savoring his triumph; waited while we crouched and watched them at their work.

One of the men below was Mister Bowles; I recognized the angular figure, the smooth hair—he was bareheaded, curiously boyish looking. The other with him was much shorter and slighter. They were holding the statue steady as it hung there. Three of the men above were at the rope, some dozen feet to the right, along the crest of the hollow. The fourth, who was facing us, I knew at once for Mister Smith. They had rigged up a scaffold by means of three oars lashed together, and he was standing against this, using his weight as a wedge.

We could hear and see everything. The creak of the ropes, the winching sound of the pulley wheels below the scaffold, the scrape and setting of the men's feet and their grunts of exertion as they heaved together on the rope, the glinting fibers of the rope itself as it descended from the oar over-hanging the slope to the slings at the statue's shoulders—they had fashioned a rope harness for it. Everything was as clear as if it had been daylight—I could even see the brass buckle on Mister Smith's belt. The statue gazed serenely across the moonwashed spaces between us, walking on air now.

So for the space of perhaps five or six minutes we crouched there and watched: watched as the statue rose foot by foot with the pulls on the rope, beyond the reaching hands of those below, slowly upward until it was clear of the bankside, hanging free. I could see nothing of Mister Bowles except his back, but I could imagine the anxiety on his face as he watched his darling's progress upward. His helper below had stepped back from the bank and stood behind him a little.

There was a dreadful fascination in the spectacle, in this purposeful, doomed activity, in their absorption and helplessness, Mister Bowles and his helper trapped like flies in that bowl of light, the others outlined there, only the exposed slope below to escape by. Dramatic, Excellency. But it was the bronze youth himself, as they hauled him clear, who held my attention, and aroused my superstitious awe. He hung there, his head just below the top of the slope, swaying very slightly. And his ropes creaked. Excellency, I was looking at the crucified man of my childhood, but transformed it seemed, ecstatic—that raised face, that dreaming smile—triumphant in the hands of his persecutors. The moon threw his brows into prominence, shadowed the sockets of his eyes. He held out his hand toward us.

Then, abruptly, the tableau was broken by Mister Bowles. He bent down, took up a length of rope lying beside him, began to clamber up toward the statue's feet. I think he was going to rope the feet, Excellency, so that the others could draw him in horizontally the rest of the way, bring him flat onto the crest of the slope. But he was given no time. It was now, with the statue suspended there, the men above taking the strain, Mister Bowles climbing awkwardly, hampered by the rope, it was now that Mahmoud whispered the firing orders, left of him at those above, right of him at those below. If the men before us heard the click of the bolts, they had no time to move, barely time to look up, even. Perhaps they saw the glimmer of a face, the glint of a gun barrel. But the shots crashed out, and continued without pause, for what seemed long enough to destroy the world. Mister Smith dropped at once, straight down into the hollow, diving past the statue, to end quite still at the foot of the slope. He was killed outright, I think. My eye went from him to Mister Bowles's assistant, who had turned to face the shots. It was Lydia. She ran three steps forward, then fell, but she was still moving. The statue, released, dropped with a rattle of wheels, like clockwork, feet first, straight onto Mister Bowles who made or seemed to make, at the last moment, some embracing or protective gesture toward it, before it struck him on head and chest and bore him beneath it down to the floor of the hollow, where the shots masked the crash of its fall. Lydia, on one knee, the other leg trailing, crawled a little way toward the statue and the inert form lying half under it. She was shot again, lowered herself onto her face, writhed briefly as if trying to turn over onto her side, to a more comfortable position. But she couldn't manage this, and after a moment lay still.

Mahmoud shouted and the firing stopped. A series of appalling groans came from somewhere at the top of the slope. We listened to these sounds in silence for some time, then Mahmoud sent the soldiers down to recover the bodies. I went with them, Excellency, a sort of dogged self-punishing urge to completeness impelling me. I saw Lydia and Mister Smith lifted, quite tenderly now, by the sober-faced soldiers, carried to the top. Lydia's hair had come down and hung behind her as she was carried up. Her face was unmarked, a white oval in the moonlight, eyes staring. It took six men to raise the statue sufficiently for Mister Bowles to be extricated from under it. I looked at him once and then no more. He had no eyes, no nose, no mouth: only a glistening mask of blood. Mercifully, at this point I was released from further attention by an attack of vomiting. Spasm after spasm kept me there, while they made litters for the bodies with the oars and spars Mister Smith's men had brought up. Still retching, I crawled into the bushes, out of sight. No one looked for me or called my name. I lay there motionless, until the steps and voices and groans had gone, until long after they had gone.

Gradually, with the restored calm of night around me, the warm air enfolding me, I began to feel comforted. My loneliness and sickness were compounded with those of the world, diffused to the farthest spaces I could imagine. I knew that my limbs would not carry me down again. After a while, I slept, Excellency. Slept through the crossing of the moon and waning of the stars, through the first light. When I awoke I was cold and hungry, but my mind was clear. I stepped out from the bushes, looked briefly across the floor of the hollow. The statue was still there, lying face down, his back leg raised a little from the ground. The fall had broken off his right arm at the elbow, so that he was prostrate against the earth, his face pressed into it. I could not see the arm anywhere, and I did not look for it.

I climbed out of the hollow, along behind the remains of the villa. I came to the one arch left standing and the angle of the ruined wall. There was the cavity below it just as Mister Bowles had described—he had taken great care, I remembered suddenly, to describe the precise location of his "finds." Acting on impulse, I made my way up there, knelt above the cavity, put in my hand. At about the extent of my arm, my fingers touched something. I strained further and my hand closed over an object cold, smooth, *shaped*. I was excited, Excellency. I drew it out: it was a doll, made of some hard, whitish, rubbery material resembling congealed fat; a grotesquely, offensively ugly doll, with protuberant eyes and thick blubbery lips; bald, but otherwise quite sexless and ageless. In the morning sunshine I stood there, turning the obscene thing over in my hands. On its nude left buttock, stamped in faint blue ink, *Potsdam 1896*. I knew now why Mister Bowles had returned to the site that afternoon, the afternoon he had been "led" to the statue: not to complete his researches, as he had given out, but to plant this outrageous doll: he had intended Mahmoud and Izzet to find it after he had gone. It was his last trick, Excellency, quite gratuitous, designed to give aesthetic shape to his whole transaction. Did I not say he was an artist? Also, of course, it was part of his "mission," part of what he had been sent to do. He had wanted to show them the error of their ways.

After a moment more, I knelt again, carefully replaced the monstrous thing. They will look there, if they retain any belief in his truthfulness. I hope they find it—perhaps they already have; they have been busy on the site these last few days.

All that is more than a week ago, eight, perhaps nine days—I do not keep count of the days, Excellency. There were nine deaths altogether: Mahmoud's four soldiers—the two above were also killed, and in the same way, stabbed as they lay there; and five of Mister Bowles's party—the wounded man died two days afterward; he had been shot in the abdomen. The sixth, who was thought to be a Pole but turned out to be Lithuanian, was unhurt. He was found next day in the foothills near the shore. He is at present in the military prison and it is probable, with that leniency the Turks show after bloodshed, that he will be released.

It is not known for sure who killed the soldiers. Their rifles had been taken, and their bayonets, and cartridge belts, and boots. None of this was found either on the site itself or on the boat when they searched it afterward. I myself see this as proof that the murders were done by Greek rebels from the mountains. And it confirms my suspicions about Mister Smith: if he was there to land arms he would have had the means of communicating with the rebels. I think he arranged it in advance, as soon as the date of the attempt had been fixed with Mister Bowles. I would like to think it was without Mister Bowles's contrivance, but he must have had some knowledge of it, knowledge that his obsession enabled him to disregard.

Now I have his notebook only, the rows of neat figures recording his trickeries. No words, no intrusion of feeling, not even a reference to the statue. The notebook was to record his transactions only—which were also his acts of retribution. He was keeping accounts straight with his *daimon*.

Other than that, nothing. Nothing of hers, of Lydia's. They have locked up the studio until her parents in Lyon can be informed.

Nothing really but questions. Questions of fact, questions of interpretation. The head, the bracelet, the documents concerning the lease—I do not know where he hid them. Probably up there in the hills somewhere, but far away from the ruins. Someday, no doubt, they will be found again, to provide a new set of puzzles.

Mister Bowles and Lydia too remain mysteries to me—opaque, ungraspable. As does this brief action in which we were all engaged . . .

At least I did not make characters of them. Now, after these few days, they have already lost unity in my mind; their wholeness was a physical impression only, not surviving the body. I am left with fragments—that word again: Mister Bowles as he was on the day of his arrival, as he stood bareheaded, momentarily bemused, with all my story contained in his luggage—the head, the bracelet, the obscene doll; his face as he laid the head on Mahmoud's desk, that quick licking of the lips his only sign of stress; his face again, gleaming and fanatical as he ministered to the bronze youth; then that final mask of blood. There is no way now of recombining these elements.

And Lydia, whom I neglected so after the statue was found: her awareness of him right from the start, we all saw it that first evening; every movement was for him—as if she had been waiting. Her bare arm glimpsed among the rocks, her landscapes, which imprisoned things—we ourselves were arrested that day in her studio, in poses to her liking, among the other objects assembled there. Then I saw her as Circe. But there was the gown, that sacrificial smudge. I should have known then. She was the victim of all of us, because she had nothing material to gain. She was there for love, Excellency. It was as if she was waiting—as if her possession of freedom was only apparent—until Mister Bowles came. Perfect balance is insufferable, as I have said elsewhere in this report. Perhaps Lydia too, with her ostensible fear of the irrational, perhaps she too was waiting for the gesture that shatters the glass. And then, Mister Bowles had a gift for inspiring people with his own vision of things, involving them in his purposes. Like a skillful cast of the net. . . . She was intending to go with him. Their suitcases were found on the boat . . .

You will understand, Excellency, that I am offering you simply one version among many. Even in that Mister Bowles and I are alike, the version chosen being that which lends itself to the shaping fantasy at the time. Everything is thus enveloped in its own thick aura of alternatives, including me, the observer. One chooses a convenient self, a suitable standpoint. I could have been a different kind of voice in this report.

I do not know, even, what he was proposing to do with the statue. Other than getting away with it, I don't think he knew himself. Perhaps he was planning to sell it in Europe, where for an original Greek bronze of that period (if he was right) he might have got a large sum from the right buyer. I think not, but one cannot be sure. Maybe the statue itself is a fake—there would be a marvelous irony in that. It has gone by ship to Constantinople now. Izzet told me there were fragments of brain on the statue's foot, the forward one.

Mahmoud and Izzet have been obliged to leave the site—empty-handed, save possibly for the doll. There are workmen from the mainland up there. The preliminary surveys have been made. Yesterday several times, and again today, there were explosions of dynamite, resounding over the whole island. First fanfares of Herr Gesing's Commerce and National State.

I do not go up there. Since the shooting I have lived in a sort of vacuous calm. I spend most of my time alone by the shore, walking, thinking. I feel some prescience here, some demand still unsatisfied by what has been done. I sense it, glimpse it faintly, as I move toward the end; an end not seen, but contained in the beginning. Standing on the beach, among the *bric-à-brac* of ages, it is strange to acknowledge how infinitely small have been the gradations of change since he arrived on the island and my report began. Minute changes in the constitution of the sea, adjustments the wind might have made to grasses, fading of things brought about by the sun in that time. Frightening, this discrepancy, wastage of persons and hopes, blankness of endurance in things.

My hopes too, in this pang of time, have withered. "Imagine the paper work," he said. I remember his face as he said that, the look of pity in his eyes. "Abdul-Hamid is finished," he said. He was right, Excellency. I knew it then, as I know it now. My reports have not been read. Worse, they have not been kept. And now you are no longer there. It was because I knew he was right, and because of the pity in his eyes, that I betrayed him. I have Lydia's money still in the envelope, but there is no use for it now. The blood money from Herr Gesing I will not collect. I will wait here. One day they will come for me. My death will not even serve as a sacrifice; such a belated and accidental event will not be regarded with favor by any god. More than that will be required for an acceptable aroma. The world is preparing for it, Excellency.

Now you too are gone. There is nobody there. I shall bring this to a close, go for a walk along the shore, study the indifference of things. We cannot retaliate on indifference by asserting truth, only by casting doubt. Maybe none of this actually happened. Like the fly, the fly on my wrist, remember?

Lord of the world. Shadow of God on earth. God bring you increase.

ABOUT THE AUTHOR

Barry Unsworth was born in 1930 in England and graduated from Manchester University. He is the author of *The Partnership*, *The Greeks Have a Word for It*, and the much-praised novel *Mooncranker's Gift*. He has taught English in Athens and Istanbul and at present is teaching in Cambridge, England, where he lives with his wife and three daughters.